King Arthur
and
The Round Table

by
Alice M. Hadfield

CORE CLASSICS®

SERIES EDITOR E. D. HIRSCH, JR.

EDITED AND ABRIDGED BY MICHAEL J. MARSHALL,
BOB SMETHURST AND THOMAS J. KERGEL

LIBRARY OF CONGRESS CATALOG CARD NUMBER: 2001092508
ISBN 978-1-890517-35-9 TRADE PAPERBACK
COPYRIGHT © 2004 CORE KNOWLEDGE FOUNDATION
ALL RIGHTS RESERVED · PRINTED IN CANADA

FOURTH PRINTING, MARCH, 2010

DESIGNED BY BILL WOMACK INCORPORATED

COVER ILLUSTRATION BY GB McINTOSH

TEXT ILLUSTRATIONS BY HOWARD PYLE

CORE KNOWLEDGE® FOUNDATION
801 EAST HIGH STREET
CHARLOTTESVILLE, VIRGINIA 22902

www.coreknowledge.org

CORE KNOWLEDGE IS A REGISTERED TRADEMARK OF CORE KNOWLEDGE FOUNDATION

Introduction

❧

THE ADVENTURES OF KING ARTHUR AND THE knights of the Round Table were first told at the firesides of the Celts, the people whose ancestors built Stonehenge, the ring of towering stones on England's Salisbury Plain that makes a calendar of the sun and stars. From these ancient beginnings come the stories' mythic echoes. Myths are traditional stories that people have passed on since the time when they did not have writing. Often they tell how the world began, or where animals come from, or they describe a Golden Age when men were better and happier than they are now and how it happened that things turned worse. Often they tell the adventures of heroes who overcome dangers we fear to face. They

I

were one way to teach lessons, explain mysteries, and entertain as well.

The tales of King Arthur were collected and retold by Sir Thomas Malory in 1470 in his famous book *Le Morte d'Arthur*. Malory was a scoundrel who stole cattle, robbed monasteries, and probably murdered too. He spent most of later life in prison, and it was there he wrote the stories as we know them today, drawing together parts from Britain, France, and Germany. In his hands they become a type of story we call a romance. Romances were very popular in the Middle Ages, when traveling musicians sang about love and adventure, dragons and wizards, and noble knights and their fair ladyloves. Romances tend to take magical things seriously and give an air of mysterious significance to nearly everything. Miguel de Cervantes wrote his famous book *Don Quixote* largely to show how silly it would be to believe in what romances said could happen.

Even though Malory wrote a romance, and the most famous figures — Queen Guenevere, Merlin the wizard, Sir Tristram, and Sir Lancelot — are all figures from Celtic folklore, he wanted it to seem historical and true. He made his characters and settings vividly realistic and played down the importance of magic. Though they come from mythic times and are mightier and grander than we are, Malory stressed their individual personalities and made them people whose feelings and behavior we can understand like our own.

We cannot find out if there was a real King Arthur. Some people think the old legends became attached to a Celtic chieftain named Arturus, a hero at the Battle of Badon in 517, where the Britons fought off Saxon invaders, and that he led them to other victories as well. But it can't be proven.

As the hero of Malory's story, Arthur tries to rule fairly in peace and prosperity. He enlists the best fighters in Briton to join the fellowship of the Round Table. The knights are rather like the Texas Rangers or the Canadian Mounties. For the sake of those suffering under injustice, they face danger alone to enforce the law and punish the wicked.

The rules they live by are a combination of Christian and military ideals known as the code of chivalry, which even today accounts a lot for what we mean when we talk about behaving like a gentleman. Chivalry called upon knights to be brave, religious, courteous (especially to women), honorable, and loyal.

Their loyalty was owed to God, to their king, and to the lady they had chosen as their true and only love. Chivalry made love something worth dying for. These virtues were tested and proven in tournaments, where knights jousted, trying to knock each other off charging horses with lances.

At the high point of the Round Table's brotherhood, when chivalry seems to have brought heavenly ideals into earthly practice, the knights impulsively take up the Quest of the Holy Grail. The story of the quest is a spiritual fable of the path to fulfillment. The Grail is a sacred cup, thought to have been the one used by Jesus at his Last Supper. It is usually seen accompanied by a lance — the one used by a solider to stab Jesus' side as he hung on the cross. These sacred objects, called relics, were believed to have been brought to Britain by Joseph of Arimathea, the man who took Jesus' body off the cross after he died. The holy cup caused the food a person most liked to eat to actually appear before him or her, spread lovely aromas wherever it went, and could heal. Miraculous to behold and radiating a halo, the Grail seemed to offer a sight of heaven from this world. But one only gets as close to the Grail as one is pure and holy. In the end, how many knights can be truly loyal to God? Only one, Sir Galahad.

The quest sets a hundred knights roaming the roads of Britain, seeking something invisible to them. Chivalry, putting its trust in the survival of the fittest, requires a knight to look for action and to put himself at the mercy of chance. The death-defying heroes of the Round Table hurl themselves into single combat with unknown foes at an instant. Thus, the quest leads to senseless duels that leave many famous knights killed or badly wounded. The world of the Round Table begins to totter.

The love between Sir Lancelot, King Arthur's best knight, and Queen Guenevere is the pivot of its fall. Sir Gawaine of Orkney, King Arthur's nephew, accuses Sir Lancelot of plotting to become king and take Guenevere as his Queen. Thus, the family of the Orkneys opens a feud with Sir Lancelot's relatives, the family of Benwick. Camelot's bonds of brotherhood, eaten at by greed and jealousy, unravel into civil war. The spirit of revenge hacks away the body of the Round Table. To stop it, Arthur finally must kill his own evil son, Sir Mordred. Badly wounded in the combat, Arthur is taken for healing to Avalon, the island in

Celtic myth where the dead go. The Golden Age he made is gone.

Yet for a time, justice and goodness, order and love reign from Camelot, and they might again, the wise men who tell myths say, when King Arthur comes back from Avalon.

E. D. HIRSCH, JR.
CHARLOTTESVILLE, VIRGINIA

The Coming of Merlin

❦

MERLIN THE WIZARD CAUSED ARTHUR to be King of Britain. No one else knew that Arthur was a prince and that he had been given to Merlin to be watched over in secret and brought to the throne.

Merlin's boyhood is as hidden as Arthur's. Before Arthur was king, his father Uther reigned, and before Uther came Vortiger. During the reign of Vortiger, Merlin first appears as a nine-year-old boy.

In Merlin's youth the island of England, Scotland, and Wales was called by two names — Logres or Britain. The Romans called it Britain from the name of a tribe of people living in it, but Logres was the name

1

that its own people used. From the beginning it was an island of marvels, with its mysterious temple of Stonehenge, its white-robed Druids, its gold, and its pearls. The stormy seas that beat its coasts prevented traders from reaching the island easily and added to its mystery.

DRUIDS
Celtic priests and wizards.

STONEHENGE
A prehistoric circle of stones in Salisbury, England, used by ancient peoples for religious ceremonies.

In the first century after the birth of Christ the Romans conquered Britain and added it to their empire. They brought peace to the island, built roads and towns, and taught the people how to obey the laws and live peacefully together. Among the Roman soldiers were some who had been told about Jesus Christ, and they spread Christianity to the people in Britain.

Four hundred years went by. Britain prospered, but Rome weakened. Her armies had to be drawn back nearer to Rome itself, and by the year 410 the last of the soldiers left the island. By this time a great many of the British people were Christian. They had built churches and decorated them with beautiful work in gold and silver. Tales of these riches reached the people living along the coasts of Europe, where nobody was Christian. These "**heathen** men" were brave but savage and greedy, and they worshipped gods who they believed demanded that men should fight and kill each other. This belief, combined with their greed for the beautiful things in the Christian churches, urged them to raid the coasts of Britain as soon as the Roman troops were gone. The ending of winter storms was the signal for raiders from all over Denmark and North Germany to cross the narrow seas and to burn and rob the villages of eastern and southern Britain.

HEATHEN
One who does not believe in the God of the Bible.

So came dark days for Britain. Churches were robbed. Priests and other people were killed or taken as slaves. British chiefs resisted, but some were traitors who made peace with the invaders in order to oppress the people themselves. Men spoke of the days when Britain was peaceful and united under one rule. They longed for a good king who would bring back peace, order, and justice. Christianity was in danger, too, for few priests or **hermits** were left alive to teach the people.

At last one British lord named Constantine set up a little kingdom of peace and order in the southwest. People believed that he was the king they longed for.

HERMIT
Someone who lives alone and apart, often for religious reasons.

He had three sons: Constance, Aurelius, and Uther. But when he died, a Welsh lord named Vortiger arranged the murder of young Constance, the heir, and made himself King of Britain.

Vortiger was one of those lords who made friends with the **Saxons**, but he was soon to know the treachery of the invaders. One of his old allies, the Saxon Hengist, came into southern Britain with a great army and a feast was held at Stonehenge. The British lords sat down unarmed, thinking all were friends. But the Saxons hid daggers under their cloaks, and at a signal from Hengist, they fell upon the British while a toast was being drunk and killed almost every man. Vortiger was taken prisoner, and to save his life he gave away his lands and villages to the enemy instead of defending them to the death.

SAXONS
A tribe of invaders from northern Germany.

Then Vortiger escaped from the enemy camp. He fled westwards to his own land of Wales, snatching what sleep he could by day and running by night, until at last he found safety in a cave in the Welsh mountains. There the British began to gather around him to resist the hated Saxons who were slaying people and burning buildings all over southern Britain.

The first need was for a fortress. A wise man advised Vortiger to build his castle on the mount of Reir, and so he went there with his followers.

First they dug a mighty moat all around the site. Working with desperate haste they dug, cut down trees, measured and marked out where they were to build, mixed lime, and collected stones. Finally, they were ready to begin to build the wall above the moat. Each day part of the great wall was built. But each night it fell to the ground. In the morning they raised it once more; in the night again the stones fell, yet no man had harmed the wall. Thus, they labored for a week, growing more and more afraid as news came that Hengist was coming nearer.

Then Vortiger sent for all the Welsh wizards and commanded them to tell him why the wall fell every night. One wizard, Joram by name, said that if a boy who had no father could be found, and if his heart's blood were mixed with the lime of the wall, then it would stand until the end of time.

The saying was strange and mysterious, but the King obeyed it. He sent messengers all over Wales to search for a boy who had no father. Two of the messengers went to Carmarthen, and outside the town wall found a broad meadow where boys were playing. The

King's men were tired, and they sat down in the shade of a tree to rest, idly watching the boys. A quarrel sprang up, and two boys had a fight, one soon getting the better of the other. The lad who had been beaten ran off, shouting taunts as he ran: "You'll pay for this, nobody's son! I am the son of a chief. You ought to be a slave! Who is your father? You never had one!"

The King's men, startled by the cries of "Nobody's son," asked what the uproar was all about. They were told that the boy's name was Merlin. He was a slim, strong boy, about nine years old, with black hair and light gray eyes. The men took him to one of the elders in the town, Eli, who said that it was true that Merlin was said to have no father, and that his mother had become a nun. When the King's messengers had explained their business, Eli brought the mother and her son to the King's mountain stronghold.

The mother told Vortiger that she was the daughter of a Welsh chieftain, Conaan. When she was fifteen she began to fall into trances and to see strange visions, and in these visions she came to know a tall knight clad in gold. Time after time he came to her. She knew neither his name nor where he came from, whether from God or the devil. Then he stopped coming and the visions stopped also. Afterwards Merlin was born.

"Alas, I do not know any more about how he came into the world."

Magan, one of the King's wizards, told the King that the gold-clad knight was one of the creatures who live in the sky, neither an angel nor a man. They love to play tricks on people. One had taken the form of a handsome knight and deceived Conaan's daughter.

Merlin wanted to know why his history was being talked about. So the King told him the story of the falling wall and Joram's strange saying, which would mean the boy's death.

Merlin looked slowly around the group of magicians standing before the King in their magic robes and horned headdresses. He looked at the ring of warriors with their spears who guarded every way, and he was not afraid. He spoke out to the King.

"Your wise men deceive you," he cried. "I will tell you the truth about the wall and prove to you that they are lying. If I make the wall stand, give me their heads!"

The challenge was agreed to. Then Merlin cried: "Tell me, Joram, what shall men find at the bottom of the wall?"

Joram did not know.

"King, keep your promise!" Merlin cried again. "Dig the moat seven feet deeper. You will find a well-cut stone."

They dug and found the stone.

Merlin cried again, "King, keep your promise! Tell me, Joram, what is under this stone?"

Joram was silent — he could not tell.

So Merlin answered for him. "There is water under here. Take away the stone, and you will find water."

And they did so, and again he challenged Joram, demanding that he tell them what lived at the bottom of the water.

Still Joram did not know.

Merlin spoke. "King, keep your promise! Drain the water. Below live two dragons. One is milk-white and the other blood-red. At midnight they begin to fight and the earth shakes, and so your wall falls. You do not need my blood to build with."

All happened as Merlin foretold. When the moat was drained, out came two dragons, white and red. They sprang on each other and fought, but neither could kill the other. At last both dragons retreated into their holes and were never seen again.

The King turned to Joram and his seven magicians and ordered their heads cut off. Merlin now became the King's adviser. He warned him that soon young Uther would land in Devon and, try as he might, Vortiger would never escape him. Then Uther would be **Pendragon** and bring peace at last to Britain.

Then Merlin made his great prophecy: "Uther shall have a son, Arthur, who will destroy all traitors. He will be the bravest man alive and the most noble in thought. All his foes he will strike to the ground. All I have told will become true."

PENDRAGON
King.

It all happened as Merlin foresaw. Uther landed and pursued Vortiger, who ran to a castle near the River Wye. Uther filled its moat with branches of trees, set fire to them, and burned down the castle and Vortiger with it. Then Uther was king, and thus the destinies of Merlin and Arthur began to be fulfilled.

PART I

The Founding of the Round Table

CHAPTER 1

The Birth of Arthur

☙

THE SECRET OF THE BIRTH OF ARTHUR, KING of Britain, is hidden from us like the secret of his end. Although he was, as Merlin foretold, heir to Uther, no one can prove who his parents were. Those who say he was a man like other men tell the story thus.

When Uther was Pendragon, he fought continually against the invaders. One of his own subjects fought against him as well, the Duke of Cornwall. Uther sent messages to the Duke asking him to come to his court and make peace. He came and brought with him his wife Igraine, who was both beautiful and wise. The King and the Duke made peace. There were feasts and sports and merrymaking, and the King, who was not married, fell in love with Igraine.

As soon as she realized this, she said to the Duke:

WHEN UTHER WAS PENDRAGON, HE FOUGHT
CONTINUALLY AGAINST THE INVADERS.

"Husband, take me away from here at once, and let us
ride all night to our own castle." They did so, and the
King prepared to make war on them again.

　　The Duke of Cornwall manned his two chief castles
and sent Igraine to the one called Tintagel, while he

himself defended Terrabil, which was famous for its secret doors and **posterns** in and out. Uther **laid siege** to Terrabil, but he could make no headway, and from anger and love of Igraine he fell sick. Then Sir Ulfius, one of Uther's knights, went to ask Merlin for help in curing him.

He met the wizard dressed as a beggar on the road.

POSTERN
Private door
or gate.

Merlin told him that he would give the King all that he wished for if in return he would grant a wish of Merlin's.

When they returned to court and told the King this, the King swore to do as Merlin told him. Merlin then said that when he married Igraine he would have a child, and he must give it to Merlin to bring up. He promised that it would be for the good of the child. Uther agreed, and Merlin then told him what to do to win Igraine.

LAID SIEGE
To surround a
city or fortress
with an army
and attack.

That day the King left the siege of Terrabil, leaving some of his army encamped there, and rode towards Tintagel. The Duke's spies told him of the King's departure, and the same night the Duke led an attacking party out of one of the posterns, and in the fighting the Duke was killed. The news was brought the next day to the King, who was outside Igraine's castle at Tintagel. Then all the barons asked him to make peace with the Lady Igraine. The King asked Sir Ulfius to take messages of goodwill to her, and at last Sir Ulfius persuaded Igraine to meet the King. Uther asked her to be his queen, and they were married the next morning.

In time a son was born to them. Merlin came to Uther and reminded him of his promise. Heavy-hearted, the King kept his word. Then Merlin said: "I know a lord of yours who is a very true man, and faithful. His name is Sir Ector and he shall take care of your child. Let the child be delivered to me at yonder postern, **unchristened.**"

UNCHRISTENED
Without baptism, a ceremony of pouring water on someone joining the Church to symbolize the cleansing of the soul.

The King ordered two knights and two ladies to take the child wrapped in a cloth of gold to the postern gate and give him to an unknown poor man who would be waiting. This was Merlin in disguise. He took the child, and what he did then no one knows, but in time he brought him to Sir Ector and there summoned a priest and had the child baptized and named Arthur.

Two years after this event, the King fell ill. Merlin summoned all the lords together and said in a loud voice: "Sir, after your days are done, shall your son Arthur be king of this realm?"

The King answered: "I give him my blessing. Tell him that he must claim the crown or lose my blessing." Then he died, and no one knew who his son Arthur was or where he was, except Merlin, who kept silent.

CHAPTER 2

The Sword in the Stone

ℰ

AFTER THE DEATH OF UTHER PENDRAGON there was no true king in Britain. No one but Merlin knew if Arthur really existed, or where he was. The lords fought each other and each tried to make himself king. They built castles in which they themselves were safe, but from which they rode out to rob farmers and anyone who had any wealth. They tortured those who would not say where their wealth was hidden. Great was the misery of Britain. Cries went up for a true king who would protect the poor and keep justice for every man.

When Merlin knew that the time had come, he went to the Archbishop of Canterbury and said that if he would call the leading men to London at Christmastime, a miracle would prove who was the rightful king of

Britain. So the Archbishop summoned all the chief men of the kingdom to London at Christmas.

On Christmas Day they went to church. When they came out, they found in the churchyard a square marble stone, in the middle of which was an **anvil**, and into the anvil was thrust a sword. The stone gripped the naked sword by the point, and on the blade was written in gold letters: "Whoever pulls out this sword from this stone and anvil is the rightful King of all Logres." Here was the miracle foretold by Merlin.

ANVIL
A heavy block on which a blacksmith shapes metal by hammering.

Each lord tried to pull it out and all failed. Nobody could move it. News of the miracle was hurriedly told to all knights. A tournament was announced for New Year's Day, when the knights were each invited to try to pull out the sword.

All the great lords met again on New Year's Day. Among them was Sir Ector, who brought his son Sir Kay, who had been made a knight at the previous Halloween. With them rode his younger brother Arthur, who was only fifteen years old. He was not a knight and had no importance at all. Nor was he really Kay's brother, though no one but Sir Ector and Merlin knew this. He did not know it himself.

After the church service they all rode in a merry company to the tournament field. Sir Kay suddenly realized that he had left his sword behind in his lodgings. There was no time for him to go back, for he was due to take part in the young knights' tournament, so he asked Arthur to go back for him. Arthur went as fast as he could to their lodgings. But everyone had gone to see the fighting, and the house was locked. Arthur was angry and said: "I will ride to the churchyard and take the sword in the stone, for my brother shall not be without a sword this day."

He found no one at the churchyard, for everyone had gone to see the tournament. So he took the sword by the **hilt,** gave it a light, quick pull — and out it came. He jumped on to his horse, rode to the tournament field, and gave Kay the sword.

Now Kay, being a knight, knew the meaning of the sword in the stone. He recognized it at once. He unwisely thought he could deceive others about how he came by it. He went to his father and said: "Sir, look, here is the sword of the stone, and so I must be king of this land."

HILT
The handle of a sword.

Sir Ector was amazed. But he was a wise man, and he immediately took Kay and Arthur and went back to the church. He told Kay to swear how he came by the sword.

Kay was frightened now, and he said: "Sir, by my brother Arthur, for he brought it to me."

Sir Ector looked at young Arthur, remembering how strangely Merlin had brought him in secret as a newborn baby, told him to bring him up as his own son, and promised that in time Merlin would reveal who the child truly was.

"How did you get the sword?" said Sir Ector slowly to Arthur, standing by the altar in the quiet church.

Arthur told him exactly what he had done.

"Now," said Sir Ector to Arthur, "As I understand, you must be king of this land."

"I?" said Arthur, astonished. "How can that be?"

"Sir," said Sir Ector, using the title for the first time, "because God will have it so, for no man could have pulled out this sword unless he was the rightful king of this land. Now let me see whether you can put the sword back as it was and pull it out again."

"That is quite easy," said Arthur, and they all went

"VERY WELL," SAID ARTHUR, AND HE PULLED IT OUT EASILY.

outside into the frosty churchyard. There stood the white
stone with the anvil wedged in the top. But no sword was
in the anvil. Arthur went up to it and thrust the sword

back into its slit, which gripped the blade hard.

Sir Ector tried to pull it out, to see that there was no trick. He could not move it at all. "Now you try," said Sir Ector to Sir Kay, and Sir Kay pulled with all his might, but could not move it. "Now you shall try," Sir Ector said to Arthur.

"Very well," said Arthur, and he pulled it out easily.

Sir Ector and Sir Kay knelt down before Arthur.

"My dear father and brother," said the boy. "Why do you kneel to me?"

Then Sir Ector told him that he was not his own son, but that Merlin had brought him as a baby to be brought up as his son in his household. "Sir," said Sir Ector again, "I will ask no more of you but that you will make my son, your foster brother Sir Kay, steward in charge of your lands."

Arthur answered: "That shall be done, and no other man shall have the office while he and I live."

Then they went to the Archbishop and told him what had happened. At the end of the New Year's tournament, on the **Epiphany**, all the knights tried the sword and none could move it. Then Arthur, who was not even a knight, drew it out.

It was decided at last. Arthur took the sword in

both hands and laid it on the altar where the Archbishop was standing. Then he knelt down, and the best knight present was chosen to come forward and make him knight. After that, the Archbishop set on his head the crown of Britain, and wearing it, Arthur swore the king's oath to give justice to all men, high and low, all the days of his life. The people threw up their caps and shouted because a true king had come at last to pun-ish the wicked and defend the poor.

But many of the great lords were not pleased and refused to have a boy of fif-teen, of unknown parents, as king over them. They resisted so strongly that it was not until the summer feast of **Pentecost** that Arthur was acknowledged as the true king. The King took those who were not to be trusted away

EPIPHANY
January 6th, the twelfth day after the birth of Jesus, when the three wise men found him.

PENTECOST
The seventh Sunday after Easter, also called Whitsunday, when the Roman Catholic Church commemorates the gift of the Holy Spirit to Jesus' Apostles.

from their posts. Arthur knew that a peaceful reign did not lie ahead of him. There were fierce raiders from over the seas, hostile British lords in strong castles, and even treacherous men among his advisers. A heavy task lay before him in ruling the kingdom rightly, or even in keeping his throne at all.

CHAPTER 3

The Sword in the Lake

❧

A FEW WEEKS AFTER ARTHUR WAS MADE KING, he went out riding early one morning. He carried only a light sword, not the one that he had pulled from the stone. That sword still lay on the altar where he had placed it at his coronation. As he rode down a woodland path, he came upon the wizard Merlin being attacked by three men. When they saw a knight on horseback bearing down on them, they ran away.

"Oh, Merlin," said Arthur, "if I had not been here, you would have been killed in spite of all your crafts."

"No," said Merlin, "I could have saved myself if I had wanted to. You are more near death than I am."

As they went on, the track led to a fountain. Blocking the way was a knight in black sitting in a chair.

He refused to let them pass without fighting him and said it was his custom. "Anyone who does not like my custom can alter it if he can."

"I will alter it," said Arthur. So the knight got on his horse and they took their spears and charged each other. Each spear shattered in splinters on each shield. They leaped off their horses and fell upon each other with their swords. The blows rang on their armor and ripped great gashes through the leather joints so that their blood ran out. As they struggled back and forth, the trampled ground became stained with blood. At last King Arthur struck such a blow that his sword broke in two. The knight cried out that Arthur must yield.

"I would rather die than yield to you as beaten," said King Arthur, and he sprang at the knight and took him by the middle and threw him down. But the knight was a much heavier man than Arthur, and he wrestled so fiercely that he got Arthur down under him and held him helpless. As he raised his dagger to kill the King, Merlin cast a spell over him and he fell into a deep sleep. Merlin helped Arthur up, mounted the knight's horse, and they rode away to have Arthur's wounds dressed. The King was angry because he thought Merlin had beaten the knight, who had fought fairly and bravely, by

THEY LEAPED OFF THEIR HORSES AND FELL UPON
EACH OTHER WITH THEIR SWORDS.

using a spell.

"I told you what a knight he was," answered Merlin. "You would have been killed if I had not been there. There is no mightier knight than he, and after this he shall do you good service. His name is Pellinore, and he shall have two sons whose names will be Percival of Wales and Lamorak of Wales. He will tell you the name of the son of your own sister who shall cause the destruction of all this kingdom."

This was an evil prophecy, but Arthur was too young to be worried over a child who was not yet born. As they rode, the King said: "I have no sword."

"Never mind," answered Merlin, "near here is a sword that shall be yours."

So they rode until they came to a lake, in the middle of which Arthur saw a sight as strange as the marble stone and anvil in the churchyard. Rising out of the water was an arm, clothed in soft white silk, holding a sword in its hand.

"Look," said Merlin, "there is the sword I spoke of."

As they gazed, they saw a boat moving across the water with a **damsel** in it.

"That is the Lady of the Lake," said Merlin, "and under that lake is a rock. Inside

DAMSEL
A young unmarried woman.

that rock is as fair a place as any on earth, and richly kept. This damsel is coming to you, so speak well to her and she will give you the sword."

The boat drew to land, and the lady greeted Arthur, who returned her greeting. "Damsel," he said, "what sword is that, that yonder arm holds above the water? I wish it were mine, for I have no sword."

"Sir Arthur, King," she answered, "that sword is mine, and if you will give me a gift when I ask for it, you shall have it."

Arthur knew that Merlin would have warned him if the lady had been an enemy, so he replied: "By my faith, I will give you whatever gift you shall ask."

"Very well," she said. "Get into the boat and row to the sword. Take it and the **scabbard** with you, and I will ask for my gift when I see my time."

So Arthur and Merlin got off their horses, tied them to two trees, and went into the boat. They rowed across the lake to the mysterious arm, and when they reached it Arthur took the sword by the hilt. The hand let go and the arm sank back under the still water. They rowed straight back to the shore. The Lady of the Lake had disappeared. The King

SCABBARD
A sleeve for holding a sword.

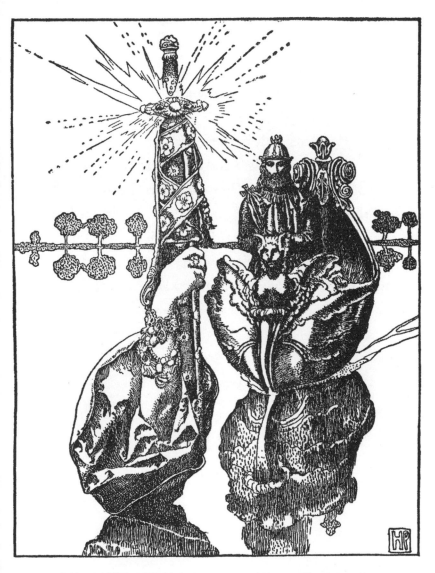

THEY ROWED ACROSS THE LAKE TO THE MYSTERIOUS ARM.

sprang out of the boat and, once safely on shore, examined the sword and saw how magnificent it was. Its name — "Excalibur" — was carved into the blade, and below it on one side was written "Take me," and on the other side "Cast me away."

Then they rode back to the court in Caerleon.

Arthur's friends were very thankful to see him, for no one had known what had happened to him. He told them all his adventures, and they were amazed that he risked his life single-handed. But all the true knights were proud to serve under such a leader who would put himself in danger like any ordinary knight.

CHAPTER 4

Sir Balin and the Hallows

ℰ

THERE WERE STRANGE AND MYSTERIOUS things in Britain in King Arthur's day — these things were called the Hallows.

The chief of them was the cup out of which Jesus drank at the **Last Supper** with his disciples and in which blood was caught from his wounds on the Cross. The second was the lance with which his side was pierced. The cup was called the Holy Grail. People said it had been brought to Britain by Joseph of Arimathea after

LAST SUPPER
Jesus' last meal with his disciples when he explained that he was about to die for the sins of the world.

33

Jesus was **crucified**. Joseph had been to Britain before. It is said that he was the uncle of Mary, the mother of Jesus, and that he made his living in the tin trade.

CRUCIFY
To kill a man by nailing him to a cross.

The fame of these things spread over Europe, and people came from many countries to see the Holy Grail. But after Joseph's death, people tried to steal the cup because they thought they could make it work magic for them, and so true lovers of the Grail hid it and kept it secret. Everyone knew of it, but no one was sure where it was. Sometimes it would appear on the altar during a service and then disappear. Sometimes it appeared in a castle hall after dinner, or to a good man while he prayed. Sometimes the lance was seen with it, its point always flaming. Sometimes angels were seen with the Hallows, along with many other wonders.

During the years of war before King Arthur won back Britain for Christianity, the Hallows were not often seen. But as the worship of Christ was restored, they began to appear again. The castle of Carbonek was their chief haunt, and its lord Pelles became known as the Keeper of the Hallows. The nearness of these holy

objects gave men unusual powers, but did not make all
men good. Pelles was a good man, but he had a brother,
Garlon, who was a very wicked man. Garlon was able to
make himself invisible, and he used this power to win
battles and kill men unfairly. He made himself the terror
of the countryside around Carbonek, until one day a
knight known as Sir Balin the Savage passed through.

Sir Balin was bringing a knight under safe con-
duct to the King, and as they rode near the town of
Carbonek, the knight reeled and fell from his horse. No
arrow had flown and Sir Balin had seen no enemy, but
there was a sound of hoofs, and in the chest of the
dying man was stuck a spear.

Sir Balin pulled out the spear and swore to
avenge the death of the knight under his protection. He
met an old hermit along the road and told him what
had happened. The hermit explained that the mysterious murderer must be Garlon, who had the power of
invisibility. Sir Balin swore to hunt him down and kill
him.

Balin soon arrived at the castle of Carbonek,
famous for the Hallows. But his mind was not on the
Hallows, but on killing Garlon. Balin was well received
and taken in to supper. He refused to part with his

sword. As he sat eating, he searched the rows of faces
intently.

"Is there a knight in this court whose name is
Garlon?" he asked his neighbor.

"There he goes," was the answer, "him with the
dark face."

Balin drew a deep breath. "Ah," he said quietly,
"is that he?"

Garlon saw that Balin was watching him, and
came over and struck Balin on the face with the back of
his hand and said: "What are you staring at me for? Eat
your food and mind your own business."

"You speak good sense," said Balin. "I will mind
my business that I came here for." And he rose up and
split Garlon's head down to the shoulders. Then he
snatched the spear that had killed the knight and
thrust it into Garlon's body.

At this killing of the lord of the castle's brother,
the hall was in an uproar. Everyone set on Balin, whose
huge figure towered over them all. Pelles thrust them all
aside and said he would kill his brother's slayer himself.
He seized a weapon, and at the first blow knocked
Balin's sword from his hands. But Balin broke away and
ran in search of a new sword, racing from room to

room and finding none. Pelles pursued him hotly. Up the winding stairs leaped Balin, and as he ran, the sounds from the hall died away and there was a deadly quiet, with only the sound of Pelles's feet behind him. If only he had a sword in his hand, or even a spear!

He flung open a door and stood amazed at what he saw. The room was hung with silks such as he had never seen. There was a bed covered with a cloth of gold, and a figure stretched silently on it; and a table of pure gold standing on four legs of silver, and upon the table was a marvelous, shining spear. Balin knew that he was in the presence of the Hallows, but the sight of the spear took all thought from him. He seized it and turned on Pelles and ran him through the thigh. There was a terrific thunderclap; Pelles fell to the ground. Crash followed crash, and the walls and roof of the castle came toppling down. The ceiling of the room fell in and buried both Balin and Pelles in the ruins.

After three days Merlin came and rescued Balin from the ruins. Merlin told Balin that the wound he had given Pelles was a dolorous blow, and that he would suffer for it, for the spear he had used was the spear with which Jesus had been pierced on the Cross, and Balin had used a heavenly object for his own earthly needs.

Merlin explained that it was Joseph of
Arimathea who lay on the bed of gold. Pelles was of
Joseph's family, and so had become Keeper of the
Hallows. The presence of the holy objects had preserved
the body of Joseph all these years. Until now the
Hallows had kept themselves apart from the world. But
Balin had involved the holy spear in an earthly quarrel.
The first results had been the wounding of Pelles, the
destruction of the castle, and a coming of sudden death
and disaster over the entire countryside.

Merlin told Balin to go away, for no one could
heal Pelles's wound for the time being. He said that the
Hallows would move among men for a time, and men
would be tormented by the glimpse of these heavenly
objects. But after years of trouble and sorrow, Prince
Galahad would come. He would heal Pelles's wound
and bring the history of the Grail to an end. But until
then there was nothing to be done for Pelles.

Balin reclaimed his sword and went on his way.
But he did not live long. That very night he arrived at a
castle. He was told that he could ride no farther unless
he fought with a knight who lived on a nearby island
and would let no one pass without a challenge. Balin

was weary, but he agreed to meet the other knight. He did not know what final grief lay before him.

"Sir," said a knight, "your shield is not good. I will lend you a bigger one — please take it."

Balin took the shield, which did not carry his own **device**, and went out. When he came to the island, he embarked his horse and himself in a boat and went over the water.

Out of the castle came riding a knight all in red, on a horse with red **trappings**. It was Balin's brother Balan, who had been searching for his brother.

He too had been tricked by the people of the castle and had been persuaded to carry a shield not bearing his own device.

DEVICE
The emblem of a person or place, a coat of arms.

TRAPPINGS
A decorated covering and harness for a horse.

He looked eagerly at the advancing knight, but when he saw the shield, he knew it was a stranger's. They charged upon each other, the two best fighters of the day. At the first shock, they unhorsed each other. Balin, weary with long riding, was badly bruised, and Balan was first on his feet. They drew swords and struck each other with tremendous blows, trampling to and fro until the ground was all mud and blood. Each gave the other seven great wounds, of which one would have killed any ordinary man. Neither of them had ever met such an enemy.

At last, the two knights collapsed on the ground, mortally wounded.

"What is your name?" Sir Balin asked hoarsely, "for until now I have never found any knight who matched me."

"My name is Balan, brother to Balin."

The world went black before Balin's eyes. He cried out, "O Balan, my brother, you have slain me and I you!"

The two brothers died side by side, Balan first, and Balin later that night.

The next morning Merlin came and took Balin's sword. He told the people of the castle that no one would be able to handle this sword but the best knight of the world, either Sir Lancelot or Sir Galahad, his son. Merlin left the scabbard on the island, and he made a bridge over to it. The bridge was only six inches wide, and no man could pass over it unless he was a knight without treachery. So the scabbard was left to await such a finder. Merlin put the sword in a red marble block that floated on water. Merlin then set the enchanted sword on its journey along the waters of Britain until the right man could handle it.

CHAPTER 5

The Marriage of Arthur and the Founding of the Round Table

❦

KING ARTHUR WAS NOW ESTABLISHED AS KING of Britain. However, his law was obeyed only in a small part of his kingdom, because invaders from across the sea held most of it. He had two chief cities, Caerleon in Wales, and Camelot in the center of southern England. A smaller town was Carbonek, on the coast of South Wales. From these castles Arthur and his knights began to wage war on the invaders, attacking them continually and giving them no peace.

For some years after he became king, the fight to restore order in Britain took up all of King Arthur's attention. But gradually he gathered good knights around him, set up a court and a government, and enforced his rule through the entire kingdom. At last there was happiness and order in cottage and castle. The fair-haired lad who had been acclaimed king that summer day in the London churchyard had grown into a bearded man, tall and handsome, stern to wrongdoers, quick and gentle to the good and to all weaker than himself or to those in any kind of need.

Now his knights begged him to marry and make his court one that would spread gentle manners and courtesy to all people. On one of his adventures, Arthur had met the Lady Guenevere, daughter of King Leodegrance of the land of Cameliard. He had never forgotten her, though he had hidden his thoughts in silence. Now he asked Merlin to go with a train of knights to the court of King Leodegrance to ask for the hand of Guenevere for King Arthur.

"This is the best news I have ever heard," replied Leodegrance when he heard the request. "I shall send him a present that will please him, for I shall give him the Round Table that Uther Pendragon gave me. When it is fully seated, it holds one hundred and fifty knights. I have one hundred good knights, but I

KING ARTHUR HAD GROWN INTO A BEARDED MAN,
TALL AND HANDSOME.

lack fifty, for so many have been killed in the wars." So
they made ready for the return journey. When King
Arthur heard that Guenevere was coming, his heart

was filled with joy. He chose his best friend and chief knight, Sir Lancelot du Lac, to ride to meet her and bring her to Camelot.

It was a fine summer morning when the two companies met. Guenevere rode on a white horse bridled with gold. She was dressed in green and gold and was more beautiful than any woman in the world. Under a blossoming appletree she met Sir Lancelot. He was in full armor, but with his **visor** up she could see his face. From that moment they loved each other, and Guenevere knew that her new life would be among friends.

VISOR
A movable part of a helmet that protected the face.

The mood of the group journeying to Camelot was all gaiety and festive. Every evening the tents were put up in a sheltered spot in a wood or valley, and supper was spread on silver dishes on the ground. The knights and ladies reclined on cushions, while musicians played sweet music under the trees and a ring of sentries kept guard. Stories were told, or one of the ladies would take a harp and sing. Slowly the light faded and the stars came out and everyone retired to their tents to sleep. In the morning there was a bustle of horses and men, of the striking of tents and wagons being packed, and off the entire company would go, chattering and laughing. Sometimes the best route was by water, when the King sent barges to meet them, and they went gliding along the river, with the notes of the harpers sounding across the water from one barge to another.

They arrived at Camelot (which some call Winchester), and there Arthur and Guenevere met again, under a canopy where the floor was strewn with flowers. The marriage and **coronation** followed as soon as possible. The Round Table was set up in the great hall and seats made for it. King Arthur had a plan for this table. He meant to have the knights who sat at it sworn to the highest standard of thought and action. It was to represent a perfect world, where love and goodness would spread throughout every vein of life in Britain.

CORONATION
Crowning of a king or queen.

When the table was ready, the Archbishop of Canterbury blessed the seats with great ceremony and set each knight in his seat, or siege. While this was being done, thunder was heard in the hall, and rolling music. Every man's heart was filled with ease and joy, and the King's face was lit by a heavenly light.

When the strange sounds ceased, Merlin, standing by the King's chair, said to the new knights: "Sirs, you must all rise and come to King Arthur to do him

ARTHUR MEETS GUENEVERE.

homage." So they rose, and while they were kneeling before the King, each man's name magically appeared in letters of gold upon his siege. Three were left empty, and over one was written: "The Siege Perilous."

> **HOMAGE**
> **Deep respect shown in a public ceremony.**

"What does this mean?" asked the King.

"Sir," said Merlin, "no man shall sit in those places but the two of best fame in any year. But in the Perilous Siege no man shall sit but one, and if anyone else is so bold as to try to sit there, he shall be destroyed — and he that shall sit there shall have no equal."

Next day was the wedding day, and at a great meeting in the morning the King arranged the ranks and grades of all his knights. His nephew Gawaine was there, son of his sister Queen Morgause of Orkney. Her husband, King Lot, had been killed by Pellinore, and she ruled in far-off Orkney with her sons Gawaine, Gaheris, Agravaine, Mordred, and Gareth. Gawaine and Gaheris were attending on King Arthur as his subjects; Gawaine was a princely and ambitious knight — while Gaheris as yet was only a **squire**.

Pellinore was also at the wedding. He was a friend of Arthur's now that he had given

> **SQUIRE**
> **A knight in training.**

up his fierce ways, and he used his strength to protect the countryside instead of attacking it. Merlin led him to the siege next to the two empty ones and the Siege Perilous and said: "That is your place, for you are most fit to sit here of any that are present."

At this Gawaine's face darkened. Later he made his way through the knights to the group of squires and drew Gaheris aside.

"That knight is given great honor," he whispered, "which makes me very angry, as he killed our father. So I shall kill him."

"Do not do it now," said Gaheris, "for I am only a squire, but when I am a knight I shall want revenge on him too."

"Very well," said Gawaine.

The King was unaware that the first split had begun at the very setting up of the table. He had forgotten Merlin's prophecy about the son of his sister who would destroy the kingdom, and Merlin did not tell him twice.

But outwardly all went well. In great splendor the King was married to the Lady Guenevere in the cathedral of St. Stephen in Camelot. Then the King established all his knights. He gave lands to the poor ones and made

AT THIS SIR GAWAINE'S FACE DARKENED.

them an equal fellowship, none above or below his
brother, as by the roundness of the table there could be
no first seat or last. He gave them a rule of life: to do no
murder or evil deed, and to be true to the King; never to
be cruel, but to give mercy to anyone who asked, on pain
of losing their place in the brotherhood of knights;

always to help any woman in any kind of need; and not to take part in an unjust cause for any threat or bribe. All the knights of the Round Table swore to keep this rule, and every year they renewed their oath at the feast of Pentecost.

PART II

The Round Table
in Action

CHAPTER 6

Sir Lancelot

꧂

THE WARS WERE OVER, BUT NOW THE HARDER work began, which was the task of governing the kingdom wisely. The King relied on his knights for help. Success or failure rested on them.

Chief of the knights was Sir Lancelot du Lac. He was the son of King Ban of Benwick, which some say was in southwest France. He was called du Lac, meaning "of the Lake," because it was said that when he was a baby he was stolen by the Lady of the Lake and brought up in her country under the waters of a lake. He had great wealth and lands throughout France. Why he chose to serve King Arthur of Britain instead of the King of France we do not know.

He came in poor clothes as someone unknown and won his fame by his own merits and not on the

WHEN HE WAS A BABY HE WAS STOLEN BY THE LADY OF THE LAKE.

strength of his family or wealth. Later on his brother Sir Ector followed him — a different Sir Ector from the one who had brought up King Arthur.

Sir Lancelot went with King Arthur on a two-year expedition into France, Italy, and finally Rome, and returned from it the leading knight in the entire country and the King's right-hand man.

No knight had ever defeated him in combat. On horse or on foot, Sir Lancelot was the champion knight of the world. He was the King's friend, and he had sworn a vow of service to the Queen. Although he would help any woman, he had sworn to be no other lady's knight but the Queen's, and to serve her and the King all his life.

Soon after they all came home from the foreign war, the King gave Sir Lancelot the task of looking after a certain part of the country and seeing that the laws were kept. He was to report on his district to the court at Pentecost.

The countryside showed the damage that had been caused by the years of war before King Arthur brought peace to Britain. For many a mile Sir Lancelot could find no castle, farm, or house where he might shelter at night. All was wildness and silence. At last he came upon some plowed land and saw buildings. The house

SIR LANCELOT WAS THE CHAMPION KNIGHT OF THE WORLD.

was built inside a protecting wall, with a gate leading in under a storeroom. He was well received by an elderly couple and given food and drink for himself and his steed. When bedtime came, his host led Sir Lancelot to the room over the gate. He put his armor and sword beside him and was soon asleep on a pile of clean straw.

Suddenly a violent knocking on the gate below awoke him. He ran to the window, and by the light of the moon saw a knight and three more riding down on him. The knight turned to face his pursuers and tackled them bravely. At this Sir Lancelot quickly put on his armor. He tied his bed sheet to the window and slid down it. To his surprise he noticed the single knight's shield as that of Sir Kay, the King's steward. He leaped at the three knights, and in seven strokes he beat them all to the ground.

"Sir Knight," they said, "we yield to you as to a champion of unmatched strength."

He answered: "I will not accept your yielding to me. You must yield to this knight, or else I will kill you."

"Fair knight, we cannot do that, because we would have beaten that knight if you had not come."

"Well, you can choose whether you will die or live. If you yield, it must be to Sir Kay."

So the three yielded to Sir Kay, and Sir Lancelot ordered them to go to the court at Pentecost and yield themselves to the mercy of the Queen, saying that Sir Kay sent them there as her prisoners.

Then Sir Lancelot knocked on the door with his sword. Cautiously the old couple peeped out through the hatch. To their astonishment, they saw the friendly face of their evening visitor, whom they had last seen going to bed in the gatehouse storeroom.

"Sir," said the old man, "I thought you were in bed."

"So I was," answered Sir Lancelot, "but I got out the window to help an old friend of mine."

Then he and Sir Kay were let in, and they all ate and drank again and went to bed in the best of spirits.

In the morning Sir Lancelot got up very early and left Sir Kay sleeping. He took Sir Kay's helmet and shield, leaving his own in their place, said good-bye, and rode off.

When Sir Kay awoke and saw the famous shield with the leopards on it, he laughed and said: "Now he will upset some of the knights, because they will think he is I and they will be bold and tackle him. While wearing his helmet and shield I shall ride in peace; no one will dare to attack me."

Sir Lancelot rode on for several days. He left behind the open country and entered a great forest. He met a lady weeping, who held his bridle and said:

"On your oath of knighthood, help my brother who is badly wounded; we cannot stop the bleeding. A

HE TOOK SIR KAY'S HELMET AND SHIELD,
LEAVING HIS OWN IN THEIR PLACE

sorceress living in the castle here told me his wound
would never be healed unless I could find a knight who
would go into the Perilous Chapel and find there a

sword and a blood-stained cloth that is laid over a wounded knight. A piece of that cloth and the sword would heal my brother if they touched his wounds."

"This is a strange thing," said Sir Lancelot. "What is your brother's name?"

"Sir Meliot of Logres."

"He is a knight of the Round Table, and I will do anything I can to help him," answered Sir Lancelot.

He followed the lady's directions and went through gloomy woods to the Perilous Chapel. He dismounted and tied his horse to the gate. As he went into the churchyard, he saw that the wall of the chapel was covered with shields nailed upsidedown, showing that their owners had been killed. His eye picked out many that he had known well at court and in the wars. His face darkened, and suddenly he was aware that below the shields there stood a line of huge armed black figures, taller by three feet than any ordinary man, and he realized that these figures had accounted for all the upside-down shields. They made no movement, but a grin of triumph came over each face as they saw another victim approaching. Sir Lancelot felt a throb of terror, but he slung his shield before him and gripped his sword and strode on.

When he was only one step away from their swords, they suddenly fell back from him. The chapel door was in front of him and he went in. The door shut behind him, with those huge figures outside, and darkness closed around him. But in a moment he made out a dim light, and going towards it he saw a figure lying under a silk cloth, with a sword beside it. Stooping down, he cut off a piece of silk. He felt the earth quake under him, and again his heart throbbed with fear.

Taking the sword, he went down from the chapel and opened the door. There were the grim figures, and as he stepped out they said: "Sir Lancelot, put down that sword or you will die."

"Whether I die or live you shall not get it from me by words or threats. Fight for it if you want it," answered Sir Lancelot. He went straight through them and not one dared attack him.

Outside the churchyard gate a strange lady met him and she said: "Sir Lancelot, leave that sword behind or you will die."

"I shall not leave it because of threats," he answered. She replied: "If you had left it you would never see the court or Queen Guenevere again." She asked him to kiss her, and he refused. She broke out in anger and amazed him by saying that all her trouble was for nothing, because she had made this chapel as a trap to catch him, and if he had given way to fear or weakness he would have fallen under her power and she would have killed him. But he had defeated all her spells.

"God preserve me from your cunning," said Sir Lancelot, and he sprang on his horse and rode away. He found Sir Meliot's sister and they hurried to the castle where Sir Meliot lay, pale and almost dead from bleeding. One touch of the silk and the steel closed his wounds and restored him to health.

Great was the joy of the brother and sister, and they did all they could to thank Sir Lancelot. Not only had he saved Sir Meliot's life, but he had broken the power of the sorceress whose spells had caught and killed many good knights. Sir Lancelot told Sir Meliot to come to the court at Pentecost and report to the King all that had happened. Then he continued on his way.

His next encounter was with another attempted trick, not of magic this time, but plain murder. As he rode under a castle wall, he heard a **falcon's** bells over his head and an escaped falcon flew into an elm tree trailing her long leashes. They caught in a bough, and as she tried to flutter off, she

FALCON
A hawk-like bird trained to hunt small game.

was jerked back and hung by the legs. Sir Lancelot was wondering how he could help her, when a lady came hurrying out of the castle and called him by name.

"Sir Lancelot! Sir Lancelot! Help me to get my hawk back! If she is lost my husband will kill me, he is so hasty. As you are a true knight, help me."

"What is your lord's name?" asked Sir Lancelot, still watching the hawk.

"Sir Phelot. He is a knight of the lord of North Galys."

"Well, madam," said Sir Lancelot, seeing that the hawk was in real danger of hurting herself, "as you know my name and appeal to me as a knight to help you, I will try and catch your hawk. But heaven knows, I am a bad climber and the tree is very high and with hardly any boughs to help me."

A little reluctantly he dismounted and asked the lady to help him off with his armor. He put it in a pile with his **arms**, and, clad only in a shirt and breeches, began to climb the elm. He reached the falcon and managed to disentangle the leashes, which he tied around a stick, and then he dropped the stick with the struggling hawk attached to it to the ground.

ARMS
Weapons.

HE REACHED THE FALCON AND MANAGED
TO DISENTANGLE THE LEASHES.

As soon as the lady had picked up the falcon, an armed man ran out from behind a bush with a drawn sword and shouted: "Aha, Sir Lancelot, now I have got you!" Sir Lancelot realized that the entire affair had been a trick, and he was caught in his shirt and without a sword. He was in much greater danger than he had been, even from the knights in the enchanted Perilous Chapel. His eye rapidly reviewed the position of the branches below him and his pile of arms on the ground. "Lady," he called, "why have you betrayed me?"

"She did as I told her," said Sir Phelot, "so there is nothing for it but your time is come and I shall kill you."

"You would be shamed forever — an armed knight to kill a defenseless man by trickery."

"That cannot be helped," answered Sir Phelot. "Do what you can."

"You will be forever shamed for this. But at least hang my sword up on a branch so that I can get it and then kill me if you can."

"Not I," said Sir Phelot. "I know you too well. You will get no weapon that I can keep you from."

Sir Lancelot began to climb down. On his way he broke off a tough spiky branch. Sir Phelot watched him, gripping his sword. Sir Lancelot measured the distance from the tree to his horse with his eye and climbed down. Long before Sir Phelot expected it, he jumped from the tree to the further side of his horse from the enemy. He had time to scramble to his feet before Sir

Phelot had run around the horse, and Sir Lancelot leaped on him and smashed the sword out of his hand with his bough. He felled him to the ground, and then, seizing Sir Phelot's sword, he cut off his head.

The lady screamed: "You have killed my husband!"

"I am not to blame," answered Sir Lancelot sternly. "You tried to kill me by lies and trickery, and now you have both paid for it." He armed himself as fast as he could, fearing that Sir Phelot's soldiers might rush out of the castle on him. He got on his horse and rode away, thanking God that he had escaped that danger.

After several other encounters, he arrived back at court two days before Pentecost.

The King and all the court were very glad. There was laughing and smiling among them, and every now and then the knights who had been taken prisoner came, and Sir Kay and Sir Meliot of Logres arrived, and they all honored Sir Lancelot.

CHAPTER 7

Sir Tristram

🥀

S IR TRISTRAM WAS THE SECOND GREATEST knight in the world after Sir Lancelot. He was born in Lyonesse, which some men say once stretched between Cornwall and France and now lies under the sea. His mother was Elizabeth, the sister of King Mark of Cornwall, and his father was Melodias, King of Lyonesse under King Arthur.

Tristram's mother died when he was born, so he was called Tristram, which means "a sorrowful birth." Melodias grieved for his wife seven years, but then married again. His new wife was jealous of Tristram because he would rule the land after his father, instead of one of her own sons. She put poison in the silver jug in the children's room, but her own son drank it and died instead. A second time she did it, but when her husband was

SIR TRISTRAM WAS THE SECOND GREATEST KNIGHT
IN THE WORLD AFTER SIR LANCELOT.

going to drink from the jug, she was forced to warn him
and so he discovered her plot to kill Tristram.

She was sentenced to be burned, but when she
was tied to the stake, young Tristram knelt before his
father and begged for her life. So she was spared and

loved the boy ever after, but Melodias thought it wiser to send him away for a while. He sent Tristram into France to learn languages and arts and deeds of arms. There Tristram learned the harp and became famous for his playing. He excelled everyone also in hunting and hawking. He combined this with his music, inventing all the hunting and hawking calls on the horns and cries with the tongue that have been used ever since. He wrote the first book describing every animal and how to hunt it. The book of hunting and hawking was called the Book of Sir Tristram.

Finally, in deeds of arms he excelled all whom he met, for he was a lover of brave deeds as well as of sweet music and noble words. When he was nineteen years old he went back to Lyonesse, and wherever he went he was loved by rich and poor.

At that time King Anguish of Ireland sent a strong knight named Marhaus to King Mark of Cornwall to collect **tribute** that Cornwall had paid to Ireland for many years. Marhaus challenged any knight of Cornwall to fight him to free Cornwall from paying the tax. No one dared to come forward, least of all King Mark. Tristram heard of this shame

TRIBUTE
A payment made from one ruler to another as a sign of submission.

and asked his father to let him go to the Cornish king to be knighted and take up the battle with Sir Marhaus. The more he was warned about the Irish knight's strength, the more determined he was, and at last he had his way.

The fight was long and fierce. Sir Marhaus wounded Tristram badly in the first charge, but the young man's strength carried him on. They fought for half a day, and then the older knight began to give ground. Sir Tristram struck such a blow on Sir Marhaus's helmet that the sword went through into his skull and stuck so that he could not pull it out. As he wrenched, a piece of the steel broke off and stayed in Sir Marhaus's skull. The Irish knight turned and ran, and Sir Tristram was the victor. He had freed Cornwall from tribute forever.

But he was very badly wounded. The spear point had been poisoned. For a month he lay near death. Then he was told that he would never get well until he went into the country from which the poison had come. So King Mark gave him a ship and all the equipment he needed, and he set sail for Ireland. As he sailed up a river, he lay in bed and played his harp, and as the boat sailed past a castle by the riverside, the King and Queen within the castle heard the merriest music they had ever heard. They hastened to the waterside, found the wounded harper, and brought him into the castle. He concealed his name because he had lately defeated the King's knight Marhaus. Tristram now found out that not only had Marhaus died of his wound, but also that he was the Queen's brother. So his life would have been short if the King had learned that it was he who had killed Marhaus.

The King had a daughter named Iseult, who was famous for her beauty and her skill as a surgeon. Tristram was given into her charge to be healed of his wound. He repaid her by teaching her the harp, and they fell in love. At the court was a noble **Saracen** from Syria called Sir Palomides, who was also in love with Iseult and half willing to be baptized for her sake, in which case she would probably have had to marry him.

A tournament was arranged while Tristram was still sick, and on the first day Sir Palomides defeated all who challenged him. So on the second day, in spite of his wound, Tristram arose. In secret Iseult dressed him all in white armor, and he left the castle by a secret doorway and suddenly appeared to

SARACEN
An Islamic warrior from the Middle East.

THE KING'S DAUGHTER ISEULT WAS FAMOUS FOR HER BEAUTY
AND HER SKILL AS A SURGEON.

challenge Sir Palomides. He came onto the field as if he
were a bright angel. He charged the Saracen knight and
brought him out of the saddle to the ground. A roar went

up from the crowd. Sir Palomides tried to withdraw from the field, but Sir Tristram forced him to stand and fight and beat him to his knees. Sir Palomides was made to promise to leave Iseult alone, and to carry no weapons or armor for a year and a day.

After this, Sir Tristram was treated well by the King and Queen and lived in great happiness for some time, hawking and teaching the Irish the hunting craft he had invented. But one day, while he was in his bath, the Queen saw his sword lying on his bed. A foot and a half from the point a piece was broken out of the edge. The Queen thought of the piece of steel that she had taken out of her brother's head before he died. She ran to her room and took the piece out of a box and fitted it into Sir Tristram's sword. It was the missing piece. In a fury the Queen seized the sword and ran on Tristram in his bath. His squire flung himself on her and saved his life. Tristram then had to confess to the King that he was indeed the slayer of Marhaus. Although the King and Iseult loved him, he had to leave Ireland. Before he went, the Princess vowed to marry no one without his consent and they exchanged rings.

He went back to Cornwall and became the fore-most man at court in fighting, hunting, and playing the

IN FURY THE QUEEN SEIZED THE SWORD
AND RAN ON TRISTRAM IN HIS BATH.

harp. Now King Mark, his uncle, was seized with that
black jealousy that poisoned his entire life. Where
Tristram was, the King would never win in jousting,

hunting, or love. He could not rest until he got rid of him.

Tristram had praised Iseult so highly that King Mark wanted to marry her. He thought that if he sent Tristram back to Ireland, he would be killed by some of Marhaus's relatives. So King Mark sent him to ask King Anguish for the hand of Iseult and to bring her back to Cornwall to his court.

The young man set out. His ship was driven by a storm back to the English coast near Camelot. There he learned that King Anguish had arrived to answer a charge of treason before King Arthur and could find no one to be his champion and fight for him. King Arthur's champion was Sir Blamore, a cousin of Sir Lancelot and a famous fighter. Tristram seized the chance to repay the Irish King for his hospitality in Ireland and offered to fight for him. He defeated Sir Blamore, who refused to yield and demanded to be killed, but Tristram would not kill him because he was of the family of Sir Lancelot, whom he admired more than any man in the world. For that, all the blood relatives of Sir Lancelot loved Sir Tristram forever.

In great rejoicing, King Anguish and Sir Tristram sped to Ireland, where once again he found Iseult. When he asked her father for her hand for his

TRISTRAM WENT BACK TO CORNWALL AND BECAME THE
FOREMOST MAN AT COURT AT PLAYING THE HARP.

uncle, the King said he wished it had been for himself.
But he had given his word to King Mark and he would
not break it. So Iseult made ready to sail with Sir

Tristram to marry King Mark.

She took with her a noble lady named Bragwaine. The Queen secretly gave Bragwaine a love potion that Iseult and Mark were to drink on their wedding day. It would make them love each other forever. On the journey, when Tristram and Iseult were down below in the cabin, they saw a gold flask containing what they thought was wine. It was the Queen's magic drink. Laughing, they said:

"Here is some special wine Bragwaine has been keeping for herself. Let us taste it."

So they drank it and thought that no drink they had ever tasted was so sweet and good. The magic potion worked in them and caused them to be in love with each other forever.

They arrived in Cornwall, and King Mark and Iseult were married. Soon afterwards, Sir Tristram left Cornwall and went to Brittany. There he served Duke Hoel and became the leading knight in the land. But he was restless and returned to Britain. He landed in bad weather on an island off the coast of Wales. He met a knight, Sir Brandiles, who told him that the Round Table desired his fellowship, for he was considered second only to Sir Lancelot. Sir Tristram served no one and held

THE MAGIC POTION CAUSED THEM TO BE
IN LOVE WITH EACH OTHER FOREVER.

no vows of chivalry, and it was felt that he should. But
something held him back. King Arthur was in Wales at
the time and was trapped in an ambush. Sir Tristram res-

cued him, but when the King asked his name he answered that he was a "poor, adventurous knight" and would not take the chance to join the King.

But as time went by, the fame of the Round Table increased, and its deeds were on every man's lips. Not to serve the King became a sign of not being a true knight, while to be made a member of the Round Table became the ideal of knighthood. Sir Tristram finally decided to see if King Arthur would accept him.

The biggest tournament of the year was held by King Arthur at the Castle of Maidens. Every knight of fame was there, wearing his colors and his arms. Sir Tristram came in disguise, carrying a plain black shield and refusing to give his name. On the first day of the tournament, he overthrew every knight who opposed him. At the end of the day, when the prizes were awarded and he was victor, he rode away and hid in the forest. The next day he returned to the fighting. He found Sir Palomides on King Arthur's side, so he joined the other side. On the third day all the spectators were shouting for the knight with the black shield, and Sir Tristram surpassed all his former victories. King Arthur and Sir Palomides attacked him together. He dealt his old Saracen enemy three tremendous blows on the helmet,

shouting with each blow: "Take that for Sir Tristram."
Then he forced his horse right up to Sir Palomides,
seized him with both hands by the neck, and dragged
him from his horse on to his own saddle, and so rode
with him a short way and flung him on the ground. The
entire field roared with cheers.

Then Sir Lancelot cried: "Knight with the black
shield, make ready to joust with me," and the highest
test of all was on Sir Tristram. At the first charge, Sir
Lancelot's spear gave him a wound that nearly killed
him. But Tristram kept his seat in the saddle and so the
spear broke off. Seizing his sword with his remaining
strength, he smote Sir Lancelot three great blows on the
helmet and could do no more. Blindly he rode off the
field into the forest.

The King and Sir Lancelot sent out search parties
for the knight with the black shield. He was nowhere to
be found. Sir Lancelot and nine others swore a vow not
to rest until they had found him and brought him before
the King at Camelot.

When Sir Tristram was well again, he set out in
search of Sir Lancelot, who would bring him to the King.
He did not know that Sir Lancelot was also looking for
him. He went to the tournament at the Castle of the

Hard Rock, hoping at last to meet him. Instead, he found an attack being made on Sir Palomides by nine knights, led by Sir Breuse Sance Pitie. It was not a fair fight, and without hesitation Sir Tristram went to the help of the Saracen. No one could resist his blows and the nine knights fled. Then Sir Tristram would have fought Sir Palomides again, but he saw he was too exhausted from the battle with the nine. So they made an agreement to meet in a **fortnight** to fight their quarrel out.

On the appointed day Sir Tristram rode into the meadow. He met a knight riding all in white armor and white colors and took him to be Sir Palomides. They advanced and fought. After a few strokes Sir Tristram knew that a mightier man than Palomides was here, and he was forced to put out his utmost. Even so, for hours he could make no headway, though neither did he give ground. Then Tristram asked the strange knight his name.

FORTNIGHT
Two weeks.

"Sir Knight," came the voice from within the steel helmet, "my name is Sir Lancelot du Lac."

"Alas," said Sir Tristram, "what have I done? For you are the man in the world that I love best!"

"Sir Knight," said Sir Lancelot, "tell me your name."

"My name is Tristram of Lyonesse."

"Oh, heavens!" said Sir Lancelot. "What a strange thing has happened!"

So the great knights met at last and told each other all the adventures that had led up to this meeting.

This was the end of Sir Lancelot's quest and of Sir Tristram's wanderings, for Sir Lancelot took him to Camelot to King Arthur. The King came quickly, took him by the hand, and said: "Sir Tristram, you are as welcome as any knight that ever came to this court." The Queen and all the ladies flocked to see the famous knight, hunter, musician, and the lover of the Queen of Cornwall.

So Sir Tristram was established as a knight of the Round Table, and his name was written over the seat that had belonged Sir Marhaus.

He was there at the last meeting of the Round Table on that day of Pentecost when Sir Galahad was seated in the Perilous Siege and the Holy Grail shone in the air before all their eyes. But when the knights scattered on their search for the Holy Grail, Sir Tristram was not among them. Perhaps the love potion had made him unable to leave Iseult. No more is told of him, though a legend says that one day while he was seated playing on his harp to Queen Iseult, King Mark crept up and killed him by a traitor's stroke in the back.

CHAPTER 8

The End of Merlin

❧

MERLIN THE WIZARD WAS A WISE MAN nearly all his life, but when he was old he fell into foolishness. Perhaps he trusted too much in his own power and so forgot that humility is the root of wisdom. He fell in love with one of the beautiful young ladies of the court, called Vivien, a girl young enough to be his granddaughter. He became quite crazy about her, followed her about everywhere, and told her any magic secret she wanted to know. He knew he was making a fool of himself, and sometimes he would think he should use his power to destroy Vivien. One day she found him in this mood and made him swear a magician's oath that he could never break, that he would never use any enchantment against her.

MERLIN THE WIZARD WAS A WISE MAN NEARLY ALL HIS LIFE.

Vivien had been brought up by the Lady of the Lake, who was also a sorceress. One magician seldom likes another, and Vivien had grown up to have no love for Merlin. But because he was a famous figure at court, she was flattered and excited by his attention, and she also hoped to get some magic power for herself. But after a while, Vivien became very tired of Merlin's devotions. Then she grew frightened of him and said he was a devil's son, but nothing discouraged Merlin.

Indeed, he could not be hurt from attacks by other people. He knew this, but in his visions he could also see that he was going to come to disaster. He warned King Arthur, whose faithful friend he had been throughout his reign, and shook his head when he foretold how the King would need him after he was gone.

"Since you know what is going to happen, do something about it," urged the King. "Prevent the disaster by one of your spells."

Merlin's pride in himself is what betrayed him into Vivien's hands. When the King urged him to use a spell, his eye clouded and his voice dwindled away to muttering. He became very angry and vanished in the form of a cloud.

Vivien's moment finally came. She had been storing up magic words and spells of a simple kind that Merlin had taught her, words that had power over elementary things like rock or earth. One day she was roaming in the forest of Broceliande with Merlin when

HE OFFERED TO SHOW HER THE MARVELOUS TREASURES HIDDEN
IN THE CAVE, AND SHE PRETENDED TO BE VERY EAGER.

he told her that there was a cave nearby with a small
entrance that no one would find under a shelf of rock.
He offered to show her the marvelous treasures hidden
in the cave, and she pretended to be very eager. Merlin

led her through the wood, and on the way a cloud of foreboding came over his spirit.

He was warned, but his confidence in himself was too complete. He went on and led Vivien to the entrance in the rock. The moment he had stepped inside the mouth of the cave, she pronounced the magic word that had power over rock, and the two sides of the opening sealed together behind Merlin.

Only the person who said the word could say the other word that would undo it. All Merlin's magic was useless to him in his imprisonment underground. Vivien ran from the rock in panic, and as she ran the thickets closed behind her and the way back was lost forever. Merlin is sealed up in the earth by his own folly and pride. In the shakings of the earthquakes, in the blasts of fire and water that burst to this day from the earth, the master of magicians groans and tries to soothe his unhappy heart.

PART III

The Quest of the Grail

CHAPTER 9

The Birth of Galahad

A HERMIT CAME INTO THE GREAT HALL AT Camelot one day when King Arthur was holding high court for the feast. The King loved to talk with wise men, so while the meal was served the hermit stood by him and uttered **prophecies**. He pointed to the Siege Perilous and asked if the King knew who would sit there.

"No," said the King, looking around at his knights, who all shook their heads, "we know not."

PROPHECIES
Mystical predictions of the future.

"I know," replied the hermit. "He that shall sit there is not yet born, but this year he will be born. He will sit in the Siege Perilous and win the Holy Grail."

Folding his arms, the hermit then stalked out

with a slow and stately tread. It was a disappointment to everyone that the adventure of the Siege Perilous was not going to happen for so long, since the person who would sit in it was not even born. Sir Lancelot, who was used to being called the best knight in the world, was secretly relieved that the siege was not for him. He did not know how closely his fate was linked with it.

After the feast, he rode out as usual on a quest to keep order in the countryside. His quest took him to Carbonek, where he had not been for a long time. Scarcely had he ridden under the gate of the town, when the people came crowding around his horse and led him into the main square in front of the tower shouting, "Welcome, Sir Lancelot, first among knights! For you shall help us out of danger!"

"What do you mean?" exclaimed Sir Lancelot.

One man stood forward, and with his hand on the great charger's neck said: "Ah, fair knight, within this tower there is an unhappy lady who has been there in pain many winters, for she is always sitting in scalding water. We know that you can rescue her."

"Well," said he, "tell me what I must do."

So they took him into the tower, up the stone stairs to an iron door that they unbolted, and made him go inside into a room full of scalding steam. There he found a young woman sitting naked in a tub of boiling water. He took her by the hand and out she stepped. She told him that Queen Morgan Le Fay had put her in boiling water by a spell because she was called the most beautiful woman in the land. No one could undo the spell except the best knight in the world, and she had been there for five years. She was Elaine, daughter of Pelles, ruler of Carbonek and Keeper of the Hallows.

When she had dressed, Elaine went with her ladies and Sir Lancelot to the chapel to give thanks to God. She had already fallen in love with Sir Lancelot, and she remained in love with him all her life. She knew that she had not the least chance of marrying him because he loved no one but the Queen. And although she had suffered so much under an enchantment in the last five years, she was not above trying enchantment on Sir Lancelot to get him to marry her.

On coming out of the chapel, Sir Lancelot was met by another group of townspeople who said: "Sir Knight, since you have delivered this lady, deliver us also from a serpent that is here in a tomb."

"Sirs," he answered, smiling, "show me the

tomb, and I will do what I can."

On the tomb was an inscription that said: "Here shall come a leopard of king's blood and he will slay this serpent. And this leopard will father a lion who will surpass all other knights." Sir Lancelot read this and said nothing. He was a king's son, son of King Ban of Benwick, and his shield was painted with leopards.

Sword in hand, he raised the lid of the tomb. Out reared a dragon spitting fire out of its mouth. Everyone screamed. Sir Lancelot struck at it, but its scaly skin deflected the blade, and its fire drove him back. Holding his shield before him to keep off the fiery breath, he sprang in and cut and sprang out of reach again, and so on for a long time. Elaine watched every stroke, noting the immense strength, the concentration of eye and hand and foot, and the fury with which he flung himself into the battle. No other fighter could compare with Sir Lancelot in action.

Elaine decided on her enchantment. After a long struggle, Sir Lancelot killed the dragon. It occurred to him that the inscription on the tomb was definitely about him, though he did not understand it.

Pelles gave a feast to celebrate two such deeds of rescue in one day. The doors of the hall were thrown open and the people of the little town crowded in to stare at the famous knight, a visitor from the great world and the foremost knight in Christendom. Dressed in scarlet, with white **ermine** and gold upon it, the mighty figure of Sir Lancelot dominated the table. Yet he was as courteous to the least as to the highest, his eyes and face as attentive to the youngest as to Pelles or the Lady Elaine. He did not show off or boast, but treated every one as his brother and equal. During that dinner, there was not a man who would not have died for him, nor a woman who was not in love with him.

ERMINE
A weasel whose fur turns white in winter; used to trim clothing.

This was Carbonek, the place of the Hallows. In such power of love there, the Holy Grail was almost certain to appear, and so it did. A dove flew in at a window swinging a golden **censer** in her beak, and the hall was filled with the most delicious smell in the world, and on the tables appeared every meat and drink that each person liked best. This was followed by the appearance of a young girl, bearing in her hands a golden vessel. Immediately Pelles, the Keeper of the Hallows, knelt down, and so did everyone in the hall.

CENSER
A container for burning incense in.

After a time the girl and the holy vessel vanished.

Everyone got up.

"What does all this mean?" asked Sir Lancelot.

"Sir," said the King, "You have seen the Holy Grail here."

Meanwhile Elaine had been busy. Her lady-in-waiting, Brisen, was an enchantress, and she agreed to help Elaine's plan. She put a spell on Sir Lancelot and gave him a magic cup of wine after dinner that made him do anything she wanted. That night Sir Lancelot married Elaine, not knowing what he did. They went to bed in a room where every window had been blocked to keep out any ray of light, for the enchantment only worked in the dark.

In the morning Sir Lancelot awoke, and not liking to sleep in a room without a breath of air, got up and opened the window. As he did so, the spell was broken. He turned from the window, and to his amazement saw a woman, Elaine, in the room with him. When she told him what she had done, and he thought of the Queen, despair and shame swept over him. He believed that his strength in arms came from his being true to his vows of service to the King and loyalty to the Queen. Now he saw that he had broken his vow and lost both his love and the secret of his strength. "Alas, that I have lived so long," he said. He seized his sword and would have killed her, but his goodness stopped him. Elaine swore to him that she had done it because she loved him and would love him until she died. Even in his brokenhearted misery, Lancelot respected that. In sick silence, he dressed and armed and rode away as fast as he could.

He went back to the court and was hardly able to meet the eyes of the Queen. No word of this adventure had reached the court, and fortunately there was bustle everywhere because the King was preparing to go to war. Sir Lancelot took up his work and avoided the company of the ladies, spending his days training knights or inspecting equipment. But the preparations took a long time, and one day a rumor reached court that Elaine, the daughter of Pelles of Carbonek, had had a son whom she said was Lancelot's, and she had given him Sir Lancelot's first name, Galahad.

Queen Guenevere heard the rumor. She thought of Lancelot's vows. She remembered how unlike himself he had been when he came back to court, and how little she had seen of him all winter. Black rage came over her. She sent for him, and by the look on the messenger's face, Sir Lancelot knew that trouble was coming. The Queen was waiting for him in her private room, standing

THE QUEEN WAS WAITING FOR HIM IN HER PRIVATE ROOM.

rigid and icy. She called Sir Lancelot a traitor and a false
knight and brought up all the things that had been eating out his heart these past months and that he hoped to

hide from her. To be the father of this child, Galahad had cost Sir Lancelot his honor, his self-respect, and now the love of his Queen. Galahad was to be the best knight in the world, but in bringing him into existence, Sir Lancelot lost all that he loved and honored.

He explained about the enchantment as well as he could. It sounded very lame, but Guenevere realized that something strange must have happened and that Sir Lancelot was very much distressed. After a long and bitter conversation, the Queen excused Sir Lancelot, but that was all that could be said. Both remained equally unhappy.

At last the King's expedition was ready, and the fleet set sail, carrying Sir Lancelot away to the wars. Time passed, the months ran into years, and at last the army came home. The Queen had forgiven Sir Lancelot and welcomed him back with King Arthur as in the days before Elaine. But he was not to escape his fate. A feast was given to celebrate the return of the knights, and Pelles sent Elaine as the wife of Sir Lancelot, with a hundred attendants on horseback. The King and Queen received her, as did Sir Gawaine, the King's nephew, and Sir Tristram, and all the knights of the Round Table except Sir Lancelot. He saw her arrival from a **turret**, and watched unseen. He saw the lady-in-waiting, Brisen, who had given him the enchanted cup of wine, leading the child Galahad by the hand. He saw the royal reception that Elaine was given, and he saw the King and Queen speak to Galahad. That night Sir Lancelot was absent from dinner, and all the time Elaine remained at court he would not speak to her.

TURRET
A small tower.

Naturally this created a scandal at court. Soon it was whispered to the Queen that Sir Lancelot was only pretending to shun Elaine in order to keep in with the King and Queen, but in secret was meeting her and telling her quite a different story. In a weak moment Guenevere believed it. She sent for him and said: "You false traitor knight! Leave the court and never dare to come into my sight again."

At these words, Sir Lancelot fell senseless to the ground. When he recovered, his heart broke and his mind gave way. He flung himself out of the bay window in the Queen's room and ran into the wild woods, a mad-man, and was not healed for two years.

CHAPTER 10

The Coming of Galahad to Court

I T WAS TWENTY YEARS SINCE THE FOUNDING OF the Round Table. All that time the Siege Perilous stood empty. Sir Lancelot sat on one side of it and different knights at different times on the other. Now, unknown to anyone, the day and the knight for whom it was made had come.

On the vigil of Pentecost the entire court and the knights of the Round Table were gathered at the great feast. As they assembled in the hall for dinner, a lady came riding fast on a **lathered** horse. She hurried into the hall and went straight to the King and asked for Sir Lancelot. She said she came from Pelles, lord of Carbonek, and must ask him to come

LATHERED
Sweating.

with her into a forest. Sir Lancelot's dark eyes rested long on the lady's face. He remembered Elaine and the enchanted cup of wine. Was it another trick?

"What do you want me to come for?" he asked.

"You will know when you get there," she answered. It was not the kind of answer that a deceiving person would make up.

"Well," he said slowly, "I will come with you."

While he was getting ready, people ran to tell the Queen that he was going to see Elaine again. But the Queen was wiser now than in the days when wagging tongues could make her believe ill of Sir Lancelot. The love between them now was sure and safe from mischief. He came to take leave of her and promised to be back by dinnertime the next day. Then he rode away with his squire and the lady.

They rode fast through a forest and came to an **abbey**. A great company of nuns came to greet them and made Sir Lancelot welcome. He realized that some strange event must be about to happen. As soon as he was unarmed, twelve nuns came in, and with them was a young lad of about fifteen, the most beautiful lad that Sir Lancelot had ever seen. In his eyes was a look of natural truth

ABBEY
A monastery where monks or nuns live.

and affection, and he carried himself easily and simply. The nuns brought the youth to Sir Lancelot and said that he was Galahad. His father stood amazed, but with a deep joy. He exchanged greetings with his son while all the nuns wept. "Sir," they said, "we bring you this child whom we have cherished, and we pray you to make him a knight, for there is no more worthy man in the world from whom he could receive the order of knighthood."

"Does he wish this himself?" asked Sir Lancelot.

Galahad answered: "Yes."

"Then he shall receive the order of knighthood on the high feast."

So when midnight was passed, the entire sister-hood gathered in the chapel, and at the first hour of Whitsunday, by the light of a hundred candles, Sir Lancelot gave his son the order of knighthood. He had been tricked into marrying Elaine and so broke his knightly vow to be true to the Queen. Now he knew that he had moved on into a deeper state, where good came out of evil. As Galahad knelt at the altar step before him, Sir Lancelot felt nothing but love for him and for his birth and for the agonies of madness and loss that he himself had suffered because of it. It was the first of those states of love that Galahad was to bring about in the world.

That morning Sir Lancelot kept his promise to the Queen and returned to Camelot for the feast. As the knights took their seats at the Round Table, there was a stir of excitement, for new golden letters shone around the Siege Perilous. They read: "This siege is to be fulfilled." A staggering thought struck Sir Lancelot. Could it be that his son Galahad was the mysterious figure for whom the Siege Perilous had been waiting all these years? He would wait and see. "I suggest," he said to the others, "that this writing should be covered up until the man comes who will fulfill all this." So they threw a silk cloth over the seat and hid the writing.

Then the King gave word for dinner. But just as he was going to seat himself, a squire came running in, knelt before him and said: "Sire, down there by the river there is a great stone floating on the water, and I saw a sword sticking up out of it!" A stone, and a sword! King Arthur remembered the sword in the stone that twenty years ago had given him his throne.

"I will see this marvel," he said, and went down the castle walls to the riverbank. Everyone in the hall followed in a long procession.

On the water floated a block of red marble and out of it rose a fine sword. In its jeweled hilt was carved: "Only he by whose side I ought to hang shall take me and he shall be the best knight of the world."

The King turned to his friend Sir Lancelot, clapped him on the shoulder and said that surely the sword was his.

Sir Lancelot smiled but answered gently: "Sire, it is not my sword. I am not going to put my hand to it, for I know it is not for me. I am sure that some great thing will begin today."

The King looked around, doubtful whom to call on to attempt the sword. Perhaps Gawaine, his nephew, who was always trying to rival Sir Lancelot, would have a chance now.

"Nephew," said the King, "will you try?"

Sir Gawaine looked at Sir Lancelot and at the sword and at all the watching faces. He was afraid to fail.

"Sire," he replied, "excuse me, I would rather not."

King Arthur knew he wanted to be urged. "Sir, for my sake and at my command, try to take the sword."

"Sire, at your command I will obey," answered Gawaine. He stepped onto the bank, a splendid figure in purple and gold, his red hair shining, his face white with excitement. He grasped the sword, but it held fast. Stiff with humiliation, Sir Gawaine stepped back. The King knew that someone else must fail too, to save his nephew's pride. He called on Sir Percival, who set little store on pride. He tried and failed, and stepped back smiling. Then the King decided to leave the sword for the moment and to go back to the feast.

They all took their places once more in the hall, and dinner proceeded. Suddenly, with a clap like thunder, all the windows and doors closed — yet the light did not dim at all. There was dead silence, and every heart was afraid.

The voice of the King spoke cheerily. "Fair fellows and lords, we have seen marvels today! But before night we shall see greater ones!"

As he spoke, in came an old man dressed in white, unknown to anyone in the hall. He led with him a young knight in red armor, with only an empty scabbard by his side. Sir Lancelot's heart moved. He had seen the young knight at midnight. No one else knew him or had ever seen him before. The old man led him to the King and said: "Sire, I bring you here a young knight by whom the marvels of this court shall be accomplished."

"Sir," said the King, standing up, "you are right

HE LED A YOUNG MAN WITH AN EMPTY SCABBARD AT HIS SIDE.

welcome, and the young knight with you." The old man
helped the knight to take off his armor. Under it he wore
a tunic of scarlet linen, and the old man hung on his
shoulders a cloak edged with white fur. Then he said to
the young man: "Sir, follow me." He led him to the
Round Table, to the Siege Perilous. Everyone saw Sir
Lancelot in the next seat exchange a greeting with the
stranger. The old man lifted up the silk cloth, and the
writing on the chair had changed to: "This is the siege of
Sir Galahad."

"Sir," said the old man, "that place is yours."

In dead silence the young knight sat down. Sir
Lancelot drew a sharp breath. Nothing happened. The
lad sat easily, looking around him quite naturally at the
faces of famous knights. Then he turned and said good-
bye to the old man, who left the hall. Everyone began to
talk again, and dinner went on. But now the news was
buzzing around that the name of the new knight was
Galahad and so he must be Sir Lancelot's son. The old
story of Sir Lancelot and the tricked marriage with
Elaine was told again. People slipped out of the hall and
ran to the Queen's apartments with the news, swearing
the newcomer was exactly like Sir Lancelot. The Queen
answered: "I should like to see him; he must be a noble

man, for so is his father."

After dinner the King took Sir Galahad down to the river to see the sword in the marble rock. The Queen saw the company going out, and she gathered her ladies and went too. The King told Sir Galahad what an extraordinary object it was and how several famous knights had failed to draw the sword.

Sir Galahad looked surprised. "Sire, it is not extraordinary," he answered politely, "because the adventure is not theirs, but mine. I knew this sword would be here, so I did not bring one, but here is the scabbard." It was indeed the scabbard that Merlin had left on the island that could be reached only by a bridge six inches wide. No one knew how Galahad had won it, and he said no more about it. Galahad took hold of the hilt and drew the sword out as easily as the young lad Arthur had done twenty years ago in a London church-yard. He slid it into the scabbard and said smiling: "It is better there than in the stone." Then he took it out again and looked at it up and down admiringly. "It is the sword of Sir Balin the Savage, the great fighter," he said proudly. "With it he killed his brother Sir Balan by mistake." He went on to tell the King the story and the King smiled at Sir Lancelot, for they had known of the events Sir

Galahad spoke of before he was ever born.

But the adventures of the day were not yet over.

CHAPTER 11

How the Quest Began

A S THE SHADOWS BEGAN TO CREEP FROM THE oaks across the meadow on the long June evening, the entire company followed the King to supper, every knight sitting in his place.

Suddenly there was a terrific peal of thunder. A beam of light seven times more bright than sunlight slid into the hall and filled the entire place with brilliance. Nobody could speak and they all sat stone still.

Down the beam of light glided the Holy Grail, a cup covered in white silk so that no one could see it, nor could they see if anyone carried it. Once again the bounties of the Grail were displayed, the beautiful smell, the food and drink that delighted each man most. Down the hall went the holy vessel and then it vanished.

After a while the power of speech returned, and

the King gave thanks to God for showing them all the Grail on this feast of Pentecost. But thanks were not enough for Sir Gawaine. He struck the table and stood up. "We have had whatever we desired to eat and drink," he declared stormily, "but one thing we were denied. We did not see the Holy Grail because it was completely covered. So, I here make a vow that tomorrow, without delay, I shall set out on a Quest of the Holy Grail, and that I shall keep it up a year and a day if need be, and I will never return to court until I have seen it more openly than it was shown here."

There were shouts of agreement, and one by one the knights rose and took the same oath. Sir Lancelot knew that the motive was wrong—because it had been God's decision not to show the holy object openly to their eyes—but he also knew that the entire day had been leading up to this, and the roots of it all lay far, far back and were not for him to disentangle or deny. So he too took the vow.

As knight after knight pledged himself, King Arthur foresaw the breakup of the Round Table, the scattering of its members, and the ruin of its work in the kingdom. He foresaw all the force on the side of law leaving Britain on this Quest and evil rearing itself again. He would be old and have no band of young men to fight for right. Tears were in his eyes as he faced his nephew. "Alas! You have killed me by this vow," he said, "for you have broken the most glorious and truest order of knighthood that was ever seen in any kingdom of the world. When they leave here, I know that they will never meet again, for many will die on this Quest. I regret it very deeply, for I have loved them as my life. The scattering of this fellowship breaks my heart, for it is a long time now that we have been together."

"Ah, Sire," said Sir Lancelot, "comfort yourself. It will be a great honor to us, much more than if we died in any other way, and we are bound to die some time."

"Lancelot!" The King turned and looked at him. "The very love I have had for you all my life makes me so sad. For there was never a king who had so many worthy men as I have today at the Round Table, and that is the cause of my grief."

The King could not be comforted, and the Queen and all the court felt the same foreboding. Every woman wept and every man felt that a time of greatness was coming to an end. The entire town was stirred by the preparations for so many farewells. The Queen sent for Galahad and had a few words with him in case she never saw him again.

At last the time came for bed, though no one could rest. The King ordered Sir Galahad to sleep in the royal bed that night and be lodged like a king. After a restless night, King Arthur went early to Sir Lancelot's rooms and asked him if there were any possible means of stopping the Quest. But one of a knight's chief oaths was to be true to his promise. Lancelot pointed this out. They both stood silent and knew that the thing must run its course. Sir Lancelot put his hand on the King's shoulder, and so they stood a moment, these two close friends of twenty years or more, who had at all times been each other's first and chief support. Then they went together to join the Queen at an early celebration of Mass to mark the opening of the Quest.

After the service, a hundred and fifty knights — all of the knights of the Round Table — took leave of the King and Queen.

A long procession of knights wound through the streets to the gate, followed by cheering and weeping townspeople. The King rode with his knights for the last time, with Sir Lancelot beside him. Neither spoke, for the King's heart was too heavy for speech.

At the gate the King drew on the reins of his

horse. Out rode his fellowship of knights, the most glorious band of men in any kingdom, famous for courage
and honor. Each one saluted the King, who had created
the knighthood that had made them more than other
men. Then, one by one they spurred their horses and
rode away.

CHAPTER 12

Sir Gawaine on the Quest

✣

S IR GAWAINE MEANT WELL WHEN HE STARTED on the Grail Quest. He was proud and impatient, jealous and hot-tempered, but he was not cruel or wicked. If the Quest had brought plenty of fighting and adventure, he would have done well, whatever hardships or dangers he had to put up with. But nothing like that happened.

He set off in hot spirits, determined to dare any dangers. He rode all day and met no one. The second day and the third day he met no one, only silent woods and deserted paths. He began to be depressed and irritated. At last he saw roofs and hurried there. It was an abbey, and the monks told him that Sir Galahad had recently been there; they told him of all kinds of adventures that had happened to Sir Galahad. Sir Gawaine was angry, jealous of the new knight who sat in the Perilous Siege. How foolish he had been not to go with Sir Galahad from the beginning!

As he was dismounting, moody and disappointed, one of the monks guessed his thoughts and remarked that even if he caught up with Sir Galahad, they would not be likely to stay together long since Sir Gawaine was full of unpleasantness and Sir Galahad was not. This annoyed Sir Gawaine very much, but he was cheered by the unexpected arrival of Sir Gareth, his youngest brother, with whom he was at least able to talk about things of the court.

Next morning they rode off together. They met Sir Uwaine le Avoutre, who had also had no adventures at all, and they all three agreed to keep together, which was not the original idea of the Quest. That day they passed near the Castle of Maidens, where seven knights were on patrol. They had no quarrel with them, and they were supposed to be sworn to a holy Quest, on which it was plain that no unnecessary killing should be done, but they were so bored that they not only fought the seven, but killed them all, which was quite unnecessary.

They felt guilty about this and decided to sepa-

rate after all. That evening Sir Gawaine came to a hermitage and asked for shelter for the night. "I am a
knight of King Arthur who is on the Quest of the Holy
Grail, and my name is Gawaine."

The hermit looked at him and saw right into
his heart in a disconcerting way. "Sir," he answered
gravely, "I would rather know how things are between
you and God."

"I am quite willing to tell you all about my life if
you want me to," answered Sir Gawaine, and so he did.

When Sir Gawaine finished by describing his
battle of three against seven, the hermit said that Sir
Galahad alone had unhorsed the seven, but did not
kill them. He said that Sir Gawaine would get nowhere
by going on in this spirit, and he must start all over
again. "You must make amends for this killing," he
said.

Sir Gawaine stiffened with pride. "Sir," he
replied, "it is quite impossible for us knights on
adventures to make amends. We have enough to put
up with in the hardships we have to undergo."

"Very well," said the hermit, and said no more.

All the summer he searched England for adventures and he was completely frustrated. He met Sir Ector,

who said that he had met twenty knights who all complained of the same thing.

"I wonder where that brother of yours, Sir Lancelot, is," said Gawaine. Wherever Sir Lancelot was, things were certain to be happening.

"I have not heard a word of him," said Sir Ector, "nor of Sir Galahad, Sir Percival, or Sir Bors."

"Well, if they cannot find the Grail, it is a waste of time for the rest of us to try."

One Saturday evening in October, wet and rough, with darkness coming down early, they came to a ruined chapel by the side of the track. Although most of the roof was gone there was one section that kept the rain out, so they decided to spend the night there. They alighted, took off their saddlebags containing their provisions, and made themselves as comfortable as they could. They talked awhile, wondering where they were and how much longer it would all go on. Then they fell asleep, and both of them dreamed a dream.

Sir Gawaine dreamed that he went into a field rich with good grass and flowers. In it was a herd of bulls, a hundred and fifty black and three white. The white bulls were feeding and the black ones were not, but looked restless and uneasy. They all said: "Let us go and look for a better pasture than this." And when they began to move out of the field, he saw that they were so thin and weak that they could hardly stand. The three white bulls went too. After a time some black bulls came back, but only one white one returned.

Sir Ector's dream was that he and Sir Lancelot, his brother, took two horses and said to each other: "Let us go and seek what we shall not find." Then a man came and beat Sir Lancelot and took away his armor, made him put on a rough garment full of knots and get on to a donkey. He and Sir Ector rode until they came to a well, and both had a violent desire to drink. When Sir Lancelot stooped to drink, the water sank so that he could not reach it. He got up and went back the way he had come.

When they both awoke, Sir Gawaine and Sir Ector told each other their dreams and pondered over them.

"I shall not feel happy until I get some news of Lancelot," said Sir Ector gloomily.

As they sat talking in the dark, suddenly they clutched each other, for there in the air in front of them floated a candle, clear and steady, held by a hand and forearm, covered in red silk, with a crude bridle over the arm. The hand carried the candle past them and disappeared among the chapel ruins. A voice said: "Knights full of bad faith, you may not find the Holy Grail."

When they had recovered from their shock, Sir Gawaine said: "Sir Ector, did you hear what I heard?"

"Yes, indeed," answered Sir Ector, "I heard it all. We had better find a hermit to explain it, because it seems to me we are doing all this for nothing."

Next morning they rode on. In a valley they met a knight, who used the proper salutes and gestures and offered to joust with them. Sir Gawaine eagerly accepted the challenge. At the first charge his spear went right through the stranger's breast and came out at the back. When Sir Gawaine bent over him he spoke muffled through his helmet.

"I am as good as dead. I am of King Arthur's court and was a fellow of the Round Table, and we were sworn friends. I am Sir Uwaine le Avoutre, and I was on the Quest of the Holy Grail. May God forgive you, for everyone will say one sworn brother knight has killed another." Off came his helmet, and Sir Gawaine saw that it was true.

"Alas, that this should happen to me!" he exclaimed in despair, not thinking how eagerly he had accepted the joust.

After this, Sir Gawaine had no more heart for the Quest. He and Sir Ector found a hermit who explained their dreams and the vision. The herd of bulls was the Round Table, and the good grass and flowers were humility and patience, which are always fresh and green, and in which people said the Round Table had been founded. But the black bulls were too proud to feed on the pasture. The white ones were Sir Percival, Sir Bors, and Sir Galahad. The search for better pasture was the Quest of the Grail, undertaken by most without humility. Of the three chosen knights, only one would return.

In Sir Ector's dream, the Holy Grail was the object they could not find. But Sir Lancelot abandoned his pride and took on humility, wearing poor clothes and riding a donkey. The well was the Holy Grail, and when he saw that he could not reach it, he went back and was ready to start all over again.

The candle was the good life and the bridle was the control of oneself. The effort to control one's own will had failed in these two knights. They listened glumly. Sir Gawaine asked why on this Quest they had met with no events at all. The hermit said that their hearts were full of pride, and the Holy Grail withdrew from people like them.

"Sir, in that case it is useless for us to go on in the Quest."

The hermit answered: "That is so. There are a hundred or more like you who will get nothing out of it but dishonor."

So Sir Gawaine and Sir Ector asked the direction of Camelot and turned their horses that way.

CHAPTER 13

Sir Percival

WHEN KING ARTHUR WAS A LAD, MERLIN the wizard spoke a prophecy. He said that two brothers would come who will have no equal in valor and good living, and their names would be Sir Percival of Wales and Sir Lamorak of Wales.

Years went by and the lads who were young with Arthur grew into men around him, and the first generation of knights, among them Sir Lamorak, established order and ruled Britain. Their life was hard and rough, they were constantly on horseback and in arms. One by one the knights of the Round Table hunted out people who defied the King, and they enforced law all over the country. It was a task that took all of their time. As time went on, however, this way of living drew to an end. Gradually, order became established and the wicked

SIR PERCIVAL

were either killed or made to obey the law. The next generation of knights found a different kind of world facing them, in which they had to live well in a peaceful life without the threat of an enemy.

These young men grew up quite different from

their fathers. Thinking and acting rightly were more important to them than fighting. This was very difficult for the older knights to understand. Only a few, like King Arthur and Sir Lancelot, who had always tried to think rightly as well as fight bravely, realized that the young ones were as good as the old and were better suited to the new times. Most of the older generation simply disliked them. When Sir Percival came to court, he seemed another of the new type. Sir Aglavale brought him and asked King Arthur to make his young squire a knight. As King Arthur looked at the young man, who was so obviously different from his elder brother Sir Lamorak, he saw something in him besides the strong arm and quick eye of the fighter and answered: "For the love of Sir Lamorak, he shall be made a knight tomorrow."

So he was, but the King and all the knights thought it would be a long time before he proved a good knight. That evening at dinner, the King directed Sir Percival to sit with the unproved knights at the far end of the hall. Now among Queen Guenevere's ladies, there was one who could not speak. On this particular evening this maiden astonished everyone by coming into the hall as if she were following an angel guide. She went past all the distinguished people until she reached Sir Percival.

She took him by the hand and spoke in a clear voice: "Arise, Sir Percival, and go with me." He did so, and every eye in the hall watched them. She led him to the Round Table itself, put him by the seat on the right hand of the Perilous Siege and said: "Fair knight, take here thy siege, for that siege belongs to thee and to none other." She then fell dead. Naturally, everyone took a great deal more notice of Sir Percival after this.

It soon became clear that he was an unusual person. He saw visions. He saw all sorts of things that he did not always understand. Spiritual creatures used to become visible to him, put him to tests and disappear. Some were good and from heaven; more were evil and from hell. But he was afraid of nothing. That other world of his seemed to give him freedom from the fears of this one.

He set out with all of the knights of the Round Table on the Quest of the Holy Grail. One day he was riding with Sir Lancelot. Towards them rode Sir Galahad, who had already gone through Sir Percival's halfway world into the world on the other side that was sure and clear and heavenly. Sir Lancelot was realizing more and more that the things his son knew were more important than the quests and battles of the other knights, and that these things were the basis of King

Arthur's laws.

But when he and Sir Percival met Sir Galahad, they did not recognize him because he was disguised. They challenged him, whereupon he charged his father and unhorsed him, and drawing his sword knocked Sir Percival out of the saddle. Sir Galahad then spurred his horse and rode fast out of sight. When they were able, Sir Lancelot and Sir Percival rode after him.

On his way Sir Percival was crossing a deep valley at midday, when a party of twenty horsemen came cantering out of a thicket of trees towards him and shouted a challenge, demanding whence he came. "From the court of King Arthur!" he answered, and a yell came back: "Slay him!" He went down under a thunder of hoofs and clash of arms. His good horse was killed, and though it half crushed him, it saved him from death by trampling. In a daze, scarcely knowing if it was another vision or actually happening, he saw a knight in the armor of Sir Galahad and heard him shout, and then heard hard riding and the clash and crash of falling men in armor, and shouts of dismay and rough orders to retreat. He crawled out from under his dead horse just in time to see the red knight chasing the robbers back into the copse. He shouted, but Sir Galahad rode on.

Now Sir Percival was in a very bad state, for he had no horse. In his armor he could walk only with difficulty. He sat by the road and waited for someone to pass, but no one had a horse to spare. When it grew dark he went to sleep, and he was awoken at midnight by a woman. She called him by his name and asked him fiercely what he was doing. He answered: "I do neither good nor ill."

"If you will promise me to do what I ask some time when I shall call on you, I will lend you my own horse."

Sir Percival was so delighted with the idea of a horse to get away from this desolate spot that he agreed at once. The woman went away and soon came back in the starlight with an immense horse completely harnessed as a knight's charger. Without waiting, Sir Percival mounted and rode off. As he came out of the valley, the moon rose and the horse put on speed. Faster and faster went the drumming hoofs; hedges, streams, and open fields rushed up and were left behind. Still the pace increased, and Sir Percival realized that this was no ordinary horse, and that he was in the grip of an enchantment. He could not slow his steed, but clung to its saddle and felt the world rush by. In an hour they traveled four days' journey. Sir Percival saw a

SIR PERCIVAL REALIZED THAT HE WAS IN
THE GRIP OF AN ENCHANTMENT.

stretch of roaring water coming and knew that the horse was going to hurl him into it. Quickly he made the **sign of the cross**. The horse gave a ghastly shriek and flung Sir Percival on the ground. To his horror he saw the animal turn into a devil that went into the water crying and roaring, and where it went the water burned in a track of fire.

SIGN OF THE CROSS

A gesture made by Roman Catholic, Eastern Orthodox and Anglican Christians that traces the form of a cross between the forehead, breast and shoulders to remember Jesus's death on the cross and ask for God's blessing.

Sir Percival now saw that he was on a black mountainside ringed around by the sea. He turned back from the coast, and as he was making his way through a valley, he saw a big snake dragging a struggling young lion cub by the neck. In a moment a full-grown lion came roaring and growling and began to attack the serpent. Sir Percival went to the help of the lion and killed the snake with his sword. When the lion saw that, he instantly became friendly, and by walking around and rubbing his head against Sir Percival and purring, he did all that a beast might do to make friends with a man. The knight stroked him on the neck and shoulders. So they stayed and rested all the morning, and the lion kept him company all day, and when darkness fell, they slept together. The knight had horrible dreams and awoke shuddering, but found the lion and stroked his mane and was reassured by him.

Next day at noon he saw a ship coming over the sea towards him. As it neared land, he hurried down to meet it. It was covered in black silk, and in it sat a lady, most beautiful, dressed in great magnificence. She called him by his name and said she would bring him to Sir Galahad. He was so thankful to be rescued from this dreadful place that he never thought of questioning her. In the course of conversation he made the sign of the cross. Instantly she rose up in a whirlwind and changed into a thick swirling black cloud, screaming, "You have betrayed me." And she fled over the sea, yelling and leaving a trail of fire.

But her ship remained. Sir Percival said good-bye to the lion, went on board and set the from that grim shore.

CHAPTER 14

The Death of Dindrane

❧

SIR GAWAINE HAD SEEN IN HIS DREAM THREE white bulls who were the three knights who would succeed in the Quest of the Grail. These three knights were Sir Bors, Sir Percival, and Sir Galahad, and the only one to return from the Quest would be Sir Bors.

Sir Bors was the nephew of Sir Lancelot, and like him, he also came from France. His full name was Sir Bors de Ganis. When Sir Bors began the adventure of the Holy Grail, he slept one night in an abbey and was awoken by a voice urging him: "Make your way at once to the sea, for Sir Percival awaits you there." He got up, armed, went silently to the stables and saddled his horse, and rode out through a broken wall and heard the sound of the sea. A shape glimmered on the water, and he rode his horse down to the sand. It was a ship that glowed with a strange whiteness. All was still and silent. A **gangway** ran down on to the beach. Sir Bors went on board.

As soon as his feet touched the deck, the ship drew away from the shore, but with no sign of a crew at work. The night wind whistled past his face, and it seemed to him that the ship was flying, not sailing. He could see nothing, so he lay down and went to sleep. When he awoke, he saw a knight and recognized Sir Percival. With great joy they greeted each other and told how each was brought to that strange meeting.

GANGWAY
A path made of wooden boards.

In the meantime Sir Galahad was also being brought to the ship. He was roused, like Sir Bors, at night, by a lady who told him to take his horse at once and follow her. Sir Galahad obeyed. The lady led him through the night to the dark shore, where a ship rode in the dimness between night and morning. As he came up, the voices of Sir Bors and Sir Percival came across the water: "Sir Galahad, you are welcome, for we have waited long for you."

The lady and Sir Galahad left their horses and went on board. The knights greeted each other with great

joy and made the lady welcome, though no one knew her
and she gave no name. As the sun rose they sat and told
each other all their adventures, and ended with renewed
joy to have found each other. Then the lady turned to Sir
Percival. "Do you know who I am?" she asked.

"No, indeed," he said. "To my knowledge I never
saw you before."

"I am your sister," she replied, "daughter of King
Pellinore, and you are the man that I love most."

Sir Percival was overjoyed to have found his sister, for he had gone in search of her many times. She had
two names, Blanchefleur and Dindrane, and she was
sent now to be the guide of the three knights.

In the ship were many marvels. Dindrane
showed them a sword that made its owner unable to be
wounded or to become weary. The knights agreed that
Galahad should wear it. So Dindrane bound it on to
Galahad and he said he would be her knight all the days
of his life.

While they were resting, a voice was heard telling
them to go to the wounded Keeper of the Hallows to cure
him as soon as possible. So they set off again with
Dindrane.

The three knights and Dindrane now thought

that they were drawing near their goal in the Quest of the Holy Grail. On their way they passed a castle. A knight was on patrol outside, and at the sight of them he spurred to the highway. Instead of challenging them, he asked: "Lords, this gentlewoman with you, is she a maiden not wed?"

Dindrane smiled and said: "Yes, sir, I am."

The knight leaned over and seized her bridle rein and said: "By the Holy Cross, you shall not escape me before you have yielded to the custom of this castle."

Sir Percival moved his horse up. "Let her go!" he said. "Wherever a maiden goes, she goes freely."

As they spoke, there was a clatter of hoofs. Armed men from the castle surrounded them, and with them came women carrying a big silver dish. They all declared: "This gentlewoman must yield us the custom of this castle."

"Why," said Galahad, "what is the custom of this castle?"

"Sir, any maid who passes by must fill this dish with blood from her right arm."

All three knights instantly declared that while they lived, no such attempt should be made on Dindrane. The castle knights attacked them, and a battle

DINDRANE WAS SENT TO BE THE GUIDE OF THE THREE KNIGHTS.

began which raged until dark. A truce was called. The
people of the castle offered shelter in the castle for the
night, under guarantee of safety and safe exit next morning. Dindrane advised them to accept, and so they all
went in. The custom of the castle was then more fully

explained. The lady who owned the place had been ill for a long while of an unknown sickness. A hermit had once said that if she were anointed from that dish full of blood from a maiden who was a king's daughter, she would be healed.

To the alarm of the three knights, Dindrane, on hearing the story, offered to be bled. Sir Galahad tried to persuade her that if she lost so much blood she would die, but she only smiled and answered: "Truly, if I die for her healing I shall win great health of soul, and honor to my family; and one harm is better than two. So there will be no more fighting, but tomorrow I shall yield to the custom of this castle."

Every one in the castle made great celebrations over this, and the party was lodged like royal guests. Next morning Dindrane asked for the sick lady to be brought. When she arrived, she was in great pain and distress — but not so great as the three companions of Dindrane. The bloodletting began, and as the dish filled, Dindrane grew faint, and it was obvious her life was running out with her blood. When the dish was full she said: "Madam, I come to my death to heal you. Therefore, for God's love, pray for me." Her eyes moved from one loving face to another; all were weeping.

"Fair brother," she whispered, "I die for the healing of this lady. When I am dead, put me in a boat and let me drift where chance will lead me. And as soon as you three come to the city of Sarras to achieve the Holy Grail, you will find me there too. Bury me there, for there Sir Galahad will be buried, and you too."

Sir Percival nodded, weeping. They all gazed on each other and held her hands, and so she died. On the same day the sick lady of the castle became well.

Then Sir Percival wrote a letter saying all that she had done and put it in her right hand. Then he laid her in a barge and covered it with black silk. The wind arose and drove the barge from the land, and all the knights watched it until it was out of their sight. Then they returned to the castle, and suddenly there fell a tempest of thunder and lightning and rain, as though all the world had broken.

Early the next day the knights separated and each rode off alone. Where the city of Sarras was they did not know, nor how they should get there, though they knew that if Dindrane had spoken of it, they were sure to find it.

At about the same time Sir Lancelot, also on the Quest of the Grail, lay asleep. In a vision he was told to rise and arm and enter the first ship that he found. When he awoke, he saw about him a marvelous clear light that also entered his mind and made him happy to obey. As he rode by the riverside in the darkness, he came to a little beach, and there was a boat without sail or oar. He went on board and immediately his entire being was filled with the utmost joy and sweetness. He felt that he had everything that he had ever wanted.

When the morning light came, he found that he was in the barge where Dindrane lay.

For a month he lived in the barge, floating without sail or oar wherever the wind led, watching over the body of Dindrane.

One night as the barge rocked on a little beach, he heard a horse's hoofs, and a man came riding down to the water's edge. Sir Lancelot sat motionless. The man dismounted, took his saddle and bridle, and leaped into the boat.

In the darkness Sir Lancelot said: "Sir, you are welcome."

He heard the other draw a quick breath, and his voice came urgently: "Sir, what is your name?"

"My name is Sir Lancelot du Lac."

"Sir, then you are my father."

"Ah, sir, are you Sir Galahad?" Sir Lancelot got up, knowing that his happiness was now perfect.

For six months they lived alone together in the boat with the body of Dindrane, and the time seemed nothing to them. The boat carried them to strange islands, where they had perilous adventures with beasts and wild men. At other times they drifted and watched the sky, told each other all their thoughts, and were happy in each other's company.

But Sir Lancelot knew that a mysterious fate was waiting for his son. One morning they came around a bend of a river and saw a knight all in white on horseback and leading a white horse. Sir Lancelot knew that this strange happy time was over. The knight hailed Sir Galahad: "Sir, you have been long enough with your father. Come out of the boat, take this horse, and go in the Quest of the Holy Grail."

Sir Galahad came to Sir Lancelot and kissed him lovingly and said: "Sweet father, I do not know when I shall see you again." Sir Galahad went ashore, mounted the white horse and rode into the forest. And they were parted forever.

Sir Lancelot was driven before the wind for another month, and then one midnight the boat came to rest below a rock. In the moonlight he saw a castle built on the cliffs above and a postern gate on the rock itself. He made his way through the winding passages and halls to the chief fortress. Every door stood open, leading from silent stair to silent room.

At last he came to a door that was shut. He set his hand on it, but could not open it. He put out his huge strength, but the door did not even shake.

Sir Lancelot knelt down outside the door, for now he knew that the Holy Grail itself was within and he had come to the end of his Quest. But he did not know whether he would be allowed to see the holy object or not.

"Father Christ!" he said, "if ever I did anything that pleased Thee, Lord, forgive my sins, but show me something of that I seek." With that the door opened, and out came a brilliant clearness that spread through the castle until the place was as bright as if all the torches in the world were there. Sir Lancelot rose and would have entered, but a voice forbade him.

"Sir Lancelot, enter not!"

He knelt down on the threshold.

There was a silver table in the room, and on it the Holy Grail covered with red silk, rose red, the Grail's own color. About it were many angels holding burning candles. Before the Grail stood a man dressed as a priest. Seeing him about to fall, Sir Lancelot stepped into the room. A fiery blast instantly beat him back, and he fell to the ground blind, deaf, and totally paralyzed.

Next morning the inhabitants of the castle found him lying outside the shut door. They looked after him until he recovered consciousness. He asked where he was, and they told him that he was in the castle of Carbonek. Slowly he arose and went to greet Pelles, the lord of the castle and father of Elaine, the mother of Galahad.

Pelles greeted him with joy. He told Sir Lancelot that Elaine was dead, which grieved him. Long they sat, talking over past days and the strange times that came on them.

Sir Lancelot stayed four days as Pelles's guest before he set out on the old familiar ride to Camelot. The King and Queen Guenevere were waiting for the return of the knights who had scattered on the Quest for the Grail. Life had gone drearily for many months in Camelot, and the news was more often of knights killed on the Quest than returned in safety. The news of the arrival of Sir Lancelot ran through the palace, and at last the great knight knelt before the King and Queen.

As King Arthur held his friend's hand and looked in his face, he saw that strange experiences had happened to him. That evening the King and Queen sat with Sir Lancelot late into the night, listening to what he could tell them of his doings, of Sir Galahad, Sir Percival, and Sir Bors, the barge and the dead maiden, and the unknown worlds where he had been.

CHAPTER 15

The Achievement of the Grail

❧

THIS IS THE STORY OF THE FINAL ACHIEVEMENT of the Grail that Sir Bors told the King on his return from Sarras.

One day the three knights, Galahad, Bors, and Percival all rode out of a forest from different directions and met on a crossroads. They saluted each other and knew that the appointed time was near. They rode together to Carbonek and were welcomed by Pelles.

That night the Holy Grail appeared in the castle. The three knights of King Arthur were present, and three knights from Gaul, three from Ireland, and three from Denmark. On the silver table the Grail appeared, and before it stood an old man. "Now you have seen what you most desired to see," said the old man to Galahad. "But yet you have not seen it as openly as you shall see it in the city of Sarras. Therefore, you must go hence and bear with you this holy vessel, for this night it shall depart from the realm of Britain and it shall never more be seen here. And do you know why? Because the people of this land have turned to evil living. Therefore, tomorrow you three go to the sea, where you will find your ship ready. Also take with you the blood of this spear to anoint the Wounded King, and he shall have his health. And two of you will die in this service, and one of you will come again and tell the tale." Then he blessed them all and vanished.

The knights obeyed exactly as they were told. First, Sir Galahad dipped his finger in the blood of the holy spear and Pelles's wound was instantly healed. So the injury done by the dolorous blow of Sir Balin was cured. Then they rode down to the river and found a ship ready for the sea. They did not know where they were to go, for they did not know where the "city of Sarras" was. They had often heard of it, for it was spoken of in stories, but they knew no one who had found it and come back.

As the ship drew in beside the paved bank on the

shore, they saw the barge where Sir Percival had laid the body of his sister Dindrane. "Truly," said Sir Percival, "my sister has kept her word." Then they took the table of silver out of their ship and carried it ashore. When the Grail was safely housed, they went down to the harbor again and brought up the body of Dindrane and buried her as richly as was fitting for a king's daughter.

The lord of the castle soon heard that they had brought the Grail. He was afraid that his power would come to an end, and so he seized the three knights and imprisoned them in a deep hole. So they lived for a year; then the lord fell ill and sent for the knights and set them free. He died, and while the city council was dismayed by the problem of who should succeed him, a voice sounded among them telling them to choose the youngest of the three knights, who was Sir Galahad.

On the first anniversary of the day Sir Galahad became king, the knights as usual went early to their prayers, but this time they found the Holy Grail out of the chest and a man kneeling before it surrounded by a great fellowship of angels. The man turned to Sir Galahad who began to tremble.

Sir Galahad went to Sir Percival and kissed him. Next he went to Sir Bors and kissed him and said: "My lord, salute me to Sir Lancelot, my father, and bid him remember me."

He knelt down and suddenly his soul departed and a crowd of angels carried it up to heaven in the sight of his two friends. Then they saw a hand come down from heaven, take the Holy Grail and the spear, and carry them up to heaven. Since then no man can say that he has seen the Holy Grail.

When the Hallows were gone, the chance that all men could be both good and happy also ended. Because men had not turned to good living at the appearance of the Hallows, but had tried, like Sir Balin, to use them for personal pride or for safety, the Hallows had produced quarrelling and bloodshed instead of peace and love. So they went back into heaven and the great attempt of King Arthur to make Britain as heavenly as possible, through his knights of the Round Table, began to break down.

When the two knights realized that Sir Galahad was dead, they buried him by Dindrane, and immediately afterwards Sir Percival retired into a hermitage outside in the country and became a monk. Sir Bors was constantly with him but did not become a monk, for he meant some day to go back to Britain. Sir Percival lived a year and two months in the hermitage and then died. Sir

Bors buried him beside Sir Galahad and Dindrane.

Thus Sir Bors was left alone, in a world that knew nothing of him or his friends, of their lives and struggles and adventures. He put on his armor again and went on board a ship. He came to the realm of Britain and rode until he came to Camelot.

He had been gone so long that they had given him up for dead. He looked around on the faces he had known since he had come to the court as a young nephew of Sir Lancelot, and he saw that they were all old men. A lifetime had passed and the end had come. He stood a moment with his hand over his eyes. The King made a sign and dismissed everyone except Sir Lancelot and the secretaries. They wrote down the reports of the knights who came back from the Quest of the Grail, to be made into books that were kept in the library in Salisbury.

Night fell and the logs burned low on the hearth, forgotten as the King and Queen and Sir Lancelot sat motionless, listening. The King knew that sadder days were coming for Britain. He was middle-aged, his Round Table was broken, and the glory of the Grail was gone.

The End of the Round Table

CHAPTER 16

Sir Lancelot and the Lily Maid of Astolat

❦

THE ROUND TABLE WAS SCATTERED ON THE Quest of the Holy Grail. A few knights had returned, but the court was empty and spiritless. It was hot summer weather, and King Arthur decided to hold a tournament to keep up their spirits and their practice in arms.

Sometimes Sir Lancelot did not fight in these jousts because he always won. That discouraged the young and gave rise to tricks and foul play by the wicked. On this occasion he thought he would fight in disguise on one of the visiting teams. It was always possible to join a team on the day of the joust, and a knight could keep his helmet on and not show his face. If he had a good horse and armor and knew the rules of chivalry, he was welcome.

The tournament was to be in Winchester. The court was in London, so they all rode down through the leafy lanes and green fields of Surrey and Hampshire. On the way they lodged at Astolat. Behind them, in new armor, visor down, rode Sir Lancelot, his shield with the famous gold leopards on a blue background hidden under a covering.

Astolat was full and busy with the arrival of the court. It had a castle in which lived an old-fashioned family who did not mix much with the great world. The lady of the castle was dead, and old Sir Bernard had brought up his two sons and one daughter in a quiet simple way. The sons, Torre and Lavaine, were new knights, and the daughter Elaine was her father's darling — young, beautiful, and good, and dearly loved by all the people, who called her the Lily Maid of Astolat.

The old quiet castle did not attract the people of the court, but Lancelot rode there and was given a warm welcome, though no one knew him. When they had all made friends, Lancelot explained that he wanted to joust unrecognized, which was quite usual, and asked if he might borrow a plain shield, leaving his there to pick up on his way back. Sir Bernard said that his eldest son, Sir Torre, had been hurt in his first joust and could not go to the tournament, and that the visitor could have his shield. He asked him to take with him Lavaine, his younger son, whose first joust it would be.

The men stood talking, and Elaine listened silently, too shy at first to look much at the stranger or to speak, but gradually she began to look up at him and saw the tall, strong figure, the dark hair and suntanned face, the deep eyes that looked on all men with love. Elaine lifted up her eyes and loved him deeply, a love that was her doom because Lancelot's true love, his one and only love, was always the Queen.

The evening passed, and Sir Lancelot told tales of the King's wars. Early the next morning he and Lavaine got ready to go. Elaine came to them and asked very shyly if Sir Lancelot would wear her **favor** at the tournament. He answered that he had never done that in his life, not saying that the reason was that he was the true knight only of the Queen. Elaine replied that that would make it all the more complete a disguise for him and, moved by this idea, Sir Lancelot accepted. He tied the favor, a red sleeve sewn with pearls, on his helmet.

FAVOR
A token of affection or remembrance.

ELAINE ASKED IF SIR LANCELOT WOULD WEAR HER
FAVOR IN THE TOURNAMENT.

Sir Lavaine brought him his brother's shield and Lancelot asked Elaine to keep his shield for him until he came again. Then the knights rode away, followed by their squires.

On the way to Camelot, Sir Lancelot told Lavaine who he was. The young man gave his promise to keep the secret. Meanwhile, Elaine at home had taken the stranger's shield up to her room and had started to make a cover for it, copying the design of the gold leopards on blue in embroidery.

When the tournament day arrived, Sir Lancelot and Sir Lavaine rode out to Winchester quietly and came by a lane to a little leafy wood where the teams opposing the King were camped. Sir Lancelot was wearing the red sleeve on his helmet. They waited in hiding while the teams lined up, the trumpets blew, and the opening charges were made. Against King Arthur were the lords of North Wales and of Northumberland and many others. Sir Lancelot's expert eye followed every move. Lavaine, his lance ready, waited quivering for the word of command. One knight after another on each side charged and the battle began to take shape. King Arthur's side pressed the others hard.

"See that group of good knights," said Sir

Lancelot through his visor. "They hold together like boars chased by hounds. Now, with your help, we shall make those knights who are chasing these fellows on our side go back as fast as they are now coming forward."

He fixed his eye on the nerve center of the fight and charged right in. His first impact sent flying five knights: Sir Kay, Sir Brandiles, Sir Sagramour, Sir Dodinas, and Sir Griflet. Young Lavaine sent down two good knights: Sir Lucan and Sir Bedivere. Lancelot did not pause. That was part of the secret of his superiority in fighting. He gave no one time to recover or to think. Before half the side knew that he had joined in, he had unhorsed seven more, and Lavaine another. But in the next charge, Sir Lancelot's horse was hurled to the ground, and Sir Bors's spear pierced Sir Lancelot's side and broke off.

When Lavaine saw the horse fall, he wheeled to the King of the Scots, who happened to be unguarded, and knocked him off his horse. He grabbed the bridle and forced his way right in and held everyone off while Sir Lancelot got onto the horse. Then began a fight that no one ever forgot. Sir Lancelot thought that he would die from his wound, and he was determined to die well. Nobody could match him. He struck down Sir Bors, Sir

Ector, Sir Lionel, and three more. The first three got on horseback again and charged him. He sent them flying again and performed the final act of victory on each by taking off their helmets and proving that if he wished, he could cut off their heads. A knight so defeated was out of the battle. Forty knights did these two champions strike down, Sir Lancelot thirty and Sir Lavaine ten. The match was won, and the King and the Round Table had lost.

The heralds announced that the prize was awarded to the knight wearing the red sleeve. But the knight was nowhere to be found. At the trumpet's sound he had turned and ridden fast into the leafy wood, followed by Sir Lavaine, feeling his wound worsen as the heat of battle died away.

An old friend of his, once a knight and now a hermit and doctor, lived in the woods, and Sir Lancelot rode there fast. He was almost unconscious when they arrived. The hermit recognized him at once. He carried him in with Sir Lavaine and began a fight to save his life.

Meantime King Arthur ordered a search to be made for the victor knight. Sir Gawaine organized a hunt around Winchester, but without success. So the prize was not awarded, and the court returned to London. On the way back, Sir Gawaine happened to lodge at the castle in Astolat. The family received him eagerly and pressed him for news of the tournament. When Sir Gawaine heard their story and discovered that the knight with the red sleeve had left his shield in the castle, he begged to see it. As soon as he saw the gold leopards on the blue background, he cried out: "Sir Lancelot!"

So the news was told, and Sir Bors, who had wounded him, was stricken to the heart, for he loved Sir Lancelot more than anyone in the world. Elaine, the Lily Maid, persuaded her father to let her ride out in search of the wounded knight and Sir Lavaine. By luck she came on her brother exercising his horse in a field. She told him of Sir Gawaine's coming and persuaded him to lead her to Sir Lancelot. From then on she never left the wounded man, but nursed him day and night.

Days passed, and he lay desperately ill. Then came Sir Bors, who found him at last and stood beside the bed in such grief it made Sir Lancelot's eyes twinkle, and he said: "Cheer up, cousin. If I had not been so full of pride I would have said who I was and you would not have wounded me. Let us say no more about it."

Gradually the battle for his life was won, and at last he was out of danger. Slowly he grew better and was able to sit on his horse and do more each day. At last came the day that Elaine was dreading, when they left the hermitage and went back to the castle at Astolat. Eventually he was well enough to leave Astolat and return to court.

Elaine knew that she could not go back to her former life without him. She asked her father and her two brothers to come with her and went to Sir Lancelot.

"My lord, Sir Lancelot," she said, "I see you are really going away. Fair knight, have mercy on me and do not let me die for your love."

Sir Lancelot had never run away from difficulties in his life. He did not now.

"What do you want me to do?" he asked gravely.

"Sir, marry me," she said.

"My dear, thank you from my heart, but I am resolved never to be a married man."

"Then I shall die for love of you."

"You will not," answered Sir Lancelot. "I am twice your age, my dear, and you will grow to love me differently. You will not always feel like this. Some day you will meet a young man your own age, and all my life you may call on me to fight for you and be your knight."

"Sir, of all this I will have nothing. If you will not

marry me, I warn you, Sir Lancelot, my good days are done."

But Sir Lancelot answered: "That I cannot do."

Elaine gave a cry and fell unconscious on the ground. Her women carried her away to her room. There was silence. Sir Lancelot picked up his belt and gloves and was ready to go. Turning to young Lavaine, he asked him harshly if he was still willing to follow him.

"Sir, I will always follow you unless you order me to leave you."

So Sir Lancelot and Lavaine rode away.

Elaine lay motionless on her bed. For nine days and nights she lay without eating, drinking, or sleeping, uttering no sound but Sir Lancelot's name. Every day the people gathered at the castle gate and wept at the news that their Lily Maid was fading away.

On the tenth day she roused herself. She spoke of her love and said she did no wrong because all kinds of love come from God. She asked her father to write her short history in a letter and put the letter in her hand as soon as she was dead, to dress her in her finest clothes and lay her in a barge draped all in black, to put their old servant in charge and let the river carry her to London to the King's palace at Westminster. The court and Sir Lancelot would see her and read the letter and give her burial.

King Arthur and Queen Guenevere were sitting talking in a deep window seat overlooking the river. Into their view glided the black-draped barge, with one white figure lying in it and one old man sitting at the oars. It came to the palace steps and there remained, rocking gently. The King and Queen went hand in hand to look on the Lily Maid who lay there. Slowly the knights gathered around, and then came Sir Lancelot. The King took the letter from her hand and read it. Elaine's last message was:

"Most noble knight, my lord Sir Lancelot, now has death separated us. I loved you, and I was called the Lily Maid of Astolat. Unto all ladies I tell my sad story, but I ask you to pray for my soul and give me burial. This is my last request. Pray for my soul, Sir Lancelot."

All eyes were on Sir Lancelot as the letter ended. He told the King that Elaine's death had not been his fault and called Sir Lavaine, her brother, to prove it. "She was both fair and good, and I owed much to her, but she loved me beyond measure." When the entire story was told, the Lily Maid was carried into the palace. Next day the court attended her burial, which was performed as magnificently as for a queen. Then the servant rowed the barge home to the mourning castle of Astolat.

CHAPTER 17

The Queen and the Poisoned Apple

❧

FTER THE QUEST FOR THE HOLY GRAIL ENDED and all those knights who survived had come back to court, there was a feeling of letdown. The knights of the Round Table had waited twenty years for the coming of the knight who was to fill the Siege Perilous, and had worked hard fighting the invaders and restoring safety and peace to Britain. Now Sir Galahad had brought to an end the adventures of the Holy Grail and died, so all that was over. A new generation of invaders was prowling the coast. Many of the knights were middle-aged and the fighting all had to be done again.

The knights were in low spirits, and idle quarrels

became too important. Sir Lancelot took every opportunity to keep away from court and go on patrols. One day when he was away, the Queen gave a dinner and invited twenty-four of the senior knights. Among them was Sir Gawaine, who was known to have an appetite for fruit, especially apples and pears. Any host took special care over them when Sir Gawaine was coming to dinner. The Queen also asked Gawaine's brothers, Agravaine, Gaheris, and Gareth, and his half-brother Mordred. Together they made up the Orkney clan, who had all conspired to murder Sir Lamorak years ago. Among the other guests was Sir Pinel, who was cousin to Sir Lamorak, but who never said anything about it and bided his time for revenge. With these came Sir Bors, Sir Kay, and Sir Palomides.

If Sir Lancelot had been there, nothing disgraceful would have happened. But Sir Pinel saw his chance. He poisoned some apples and arranged them in the dish nearest to Sir Gawaine. Dinner went on, there was music, the Queen was merry. They talked of Sir Lancelot and wondered what great feat he would come back to tell about. The time came for dessert. Sir Pinel watched Sir Gawaine between the candles. But poison was a clumsy choice of weapon. Sir Gawaine was talking, and Sir

Patrise, next to him, took an apple and ate it. Then he swelled up and fell down dead.

Uproar broke out. Sir Pinel kept his head and said nothing. Everyone naturally suspected the Queen, who had arranged the dinner. Sir Gawaine was convinced that the poison had been meant for him because an apple had been chosen. Sir Bors tried to make him be quiet, but Gawaine's wild nature could not be controlled, and he stood up hotly and accused the Queen. Guenevere stood like a statue, silent, seeing it was a plot, and thinking it was aimed at her because Sir Lancelot was not there to defend her. She did not answer, so no one spoke up for her defense. Sir Mador de la Porte, cousin to Sir Patrise, challenged the Queen and accused her of the murder of his cousin.

After that, there could be no stepping back. The King was fetched, the charge repeated, and Sir Mador demanded that the queen be burned to death. The method of trial was a battle between Sir Mador and a champion for the Queen. The King was forbidden by his own laws from fighting for his wife, but felt sure that a champion would come forward, so he told Sir Mador to ask for a day for trial. Sir Mador then pointed out that none of the knights at the dinner would fight for the

SIR MADOR DEMANDED THAT THE QUEEN BE BURNED TO DEATH.

Queen, as they all believed her guilty. Sir Mador saw the
King's face change, and he immediately made the formal
request for a day for the trial. The King chose the longest
space of time that the law allowed and fixed a day fifteen

days from then. Sir Mador was to appear armed in the
meadow outside Camelot. If a champion appeared for
the Queen, God would reveal the right. If none
appeared, then the Queen must be burned. She would be
tied at the stake before the contest, ready for the judg-
ment. "I am answered," said Sir Mador, and the King
dismissed them all.

When the King and Queen were alone, they had
a desperate discussion about finding Sir Lancelot, and
what to do if he could not be found.

"What is the matter with you," said the King,
"that you cannot keep Sir Lancelot on your side?" Then
the King thought of Sir Lancelot's closest friend, Sir
Bors. True, he had been at the dinner, but he might
defend the Queen for Sir Lancelot's sake. The Queen
went that night to Sir Bors's apartments and made her
request.

He was most embarrassed by it. He had joined
with the other knights in suspecting her, and they would
think he was deliberately defending the guilty just
because she was the Queen. But when the King added
his request to the Queen's, then Sir Bors promised to
fight as her champion unless a better knight than he
should come forward. The Queen wept with relief, and

the King could say nothing, but took Sir Bors's hand and pressed it silently.

Next day Sir Bors had news that Sir Lancelot was on his way back. He promptly left the court, without taking his squire or telling anyone where he was going, and rode to meet him. He told him the entire story, and Sir Lancelot felt sure that it was a plot against the Queen. He immediately laid his plans and considered the weaknesses of Sir Mador. Sir Lancelot, like all good generals, never underestimated his enemy and tried to leave nothing to chance.

"This has worked out just as I might have chosen," he said to Sir Bors. "Now you get ready for the fight, right up to the last moment, and delay things as much as you can, because you know Sir Mador gets much too excited when there is action, and the longer he is kept waiting, the wilder he will be when the battle begins."

"Sir, let me handle him," said Sir Bors.

So Sir Bors went back to court that evening and announced that he was going to fight for the Queen. Many knights objected, as he had known they would. He answered them: "Lords, it seems to me she has always been the most generous lady with her gifts and her friendliness that I ever saw or heard of. It would be a shame to all of us if we allowed her to be burned without striking a blow for her. So I tell you all that I will not allow it, for I do not think the Queen is guilty of Sir Patrise's death. She had no quarrel with him, nor with any of us who were at dinner. I am sure that it will be proved later, whatever it looks like now, that there was treason among us."

Some of the knights came over to his side and agreed with him and some did not. So the time went on, the fifteenth morning came, and everyone crowded to the jousting meadow. The space was bare, except for one tent at each end. Opposite the royal stand, a huge pile stood ready to burn around an iron stake. There sat the Queen. In the royal stand King Arthur sat alone.

Everywhere else the ground was black with people. Never had such a crowd been seen before. Punctually on time a herald blew and Sir Mador rode on to the ground, saluted the King, and in a voice echoing hollowly through his visor, made his accusation against the Queen. The answering herald blew, and out rode Sir Bors. He saluted the King and declared the accusation false. Sir Mador, who was very wrought up, demanded to join battle at once. Sir Bors delayed with some formal appeals and held matters up for some time. Finally, they retired to their tents and took their arms and prepared. Out rode Sir Mador, lance ready, his horse's neck lathered with excitement caught from his rider. He cantered around the field shouting his challenge: "Let your champion come forth if he dare."

Hidden in the wood, Sir Lancelot watched him, noting every detail of his seat, his lance grip, the slant of his shield. He was circling a second time, the crowd was whispering, the King was glancing uneasily at Sir Bors's tent, when out from the woods there rode a strange knight bearing an unknown shield, riding a white horse at full gallop. Sir Bors rode out to meet him. There was a meeting; the stranger claimed the right to be the Queen's champion. The new knight was big and grim and rode as well as Sir Lancelot. Challenges were exchanged, the King agreed, Sir Bors withdrew, and Sir Mador faced the strange knight down the length of the **lists**.

LISTS
An arena for tournaments and other contests.

The first charge brought Sir Mador down, and the Queen's heart leaped, for in that riding and that stroke she recognized Sir Lancelot. They fought on foot, and Sir Mador struggled desperately against the grim figure that stalked after him and beat blow on blow. But at last Sir Lancelot struck him down and stood over him, unlacing his helmet to cut off his head. Sir Mador begged for his life and acquitted the Queen of his accusation.

"I will only grant you your life on condition that you never raise this accusation again, and that no mention is made on Sir Patrise's tomb of the Queen's name."

Then Sir Mador withdrew with his supporters to his tent. The strange knight walked across to the stairs of the royal stand. By that time the Queen had been released and had joined the King. They both came down the stairs, greeted and thanked the knight, and took him back into the stand for a glass of wine. As he took off his helmet there was a general shout of "Lancelot!" and "du Lac!" The King took both his hands, the Queen burst into tears, and around them gathered Sir Lancelot's family and all his friends, full of questions, exclamations, and joy.

So it all ended happily, though at one time it had looked bad for the Queen. The mystery of who poisoned the apple was not unravelled until an enchantress, named Nimue, came to court. She declared the guilty knight was Sir Pinel, and he proved her right by fleeing from court and going into hiding in France.

SIR MADOR BEGGED FOR HIS LIFE AND TOOK BACK

HIS ACCUSATION AGAINST THE QUEEN.

CHAPTER 18

Sir Meliagraunce

❦

ALTHOUGH SIR LANCELOT RESCUED THE Queen in the affair of the poisoned apple, the attempt to dishonor her had been made, and might be made again. The Queen was beautiful, and there were plenty of bad or reckless knights who would not hesitate to take a chance to kidnap her, if Sir Lancelot was elsewhere at the time.

Sir Meliagraunce, who was a coward, thought he was in love with the Queen for a long time. His love was of the kidnapping and not the knightly kind, and he waited for a chance when Sir Lancelot was away. It came on May Day. The court was in London. The Queen arranged a party to ride out into the woods and fields around Westminster. Sir Lancelot was at a council with the King and could not come, so the Queen went out without him. She was accompanied by ten knights and ten ladies. Each knight had a squire and two servants. All were unarmed, wearing green silk for May Day and carrying only light court swords.

Sir Meliagraunce lived in a castle seven miles from Westminster, and there he had many men-at-arms and archers. When the Queen was out with all her knights, out of the wood came Sir Meliagraunce with two hundred men, all prepared for fighting. He ordered the Queen and her knights to halt.

"Traitor knight," said the Queen, "what are you thinking of? Will you bring shame on yourself? Remember you are a knight of the Round Table. Think before you shame all knighthood and yourself and me."

"This fine talk is all very well," replied Sir Meliagraunce. "Madam, I have loved you many a year, and never until now could I get you at such a disadvantage. Therefore, I will take you as I find you."

At this rude speech the Queen's knights fell on Sir Meliagraunce and his men, without armor and with no hope of success. They fought with such skill that they killed forty of the enemy before they themselves were all disabled. When the Queen saw that they were

wounded and surrounded, she cried to Sir Meliagraunce
that she would yield to him on condition that her
knights were spared and were brought with her and
lodged wherever she was lodged. Sir Meliagraunce gave
way, though he had meant to kill them all and take only
the Queen, but time was passing and he was afraid some
hidden watcher in the woods might send a message to
Sir Lancelot. He meant to be safe inside his castle wall
before that happened.

Meanwhile the Queen outwitted him. While the
wounded men were being helped onto horses, the
Queen had a word with a young page, a boy of twelve,
who rode a fast fresh pony.

"When you see a chance," she said, "slip away
and take this ring to Sir Lancelot, and pray him as he
loves me to rescue me. And don't spare your horse."

The boy was on fire with pride and determina-
tion and took the first chance that came, when the big
horses were crowding across a little stream and he had to
wait until they were over. He turned his pony and
spurred down a hedge path, and though some of
Meliagraunce's men chased him, he got away.

Sir Meliagraunce knew what that meant. Sir
Lancelot would arrive. He hurried the Queen and the

knights into the castle and sent thirty archers to ambush Sir Lancelot, telling them to shoot especially at his horse, for he had no faith that even thirty of them could overcome the great knight himself. The Queen insisted on having the ten wounded knights in her apartments, where she and her ladies looked after them. Shut out, Sir Meliagraunce cursed and paced about the castle, preparing for the dreaded arrival of the Queen's champion.

The page made his way safely out of the woods and galloped his pony at full speed along the open road to Westminster. The Queen's ring won him instant admission to the palace and Sir Lancelot's apartments. The great knight was just returning from the King's council. At the words, "A page with the Queen's ring," he halted and summoned the boy. He looked closely at the ring, and as he heard the story, his color changed and one of his rare angers came over him. There was no more talking then. His armor was brought, his horse prepared, and a message sent to Sir Lavaine to follow him. Within the hour he was going as hard as the heavy charger would carry him down the road to the woods. It had not occurred to him to take a troop of knights with him; he meant to settle this alone.

Coming down to the river at Westminster, he met

a group of packhorses and drivers taking all the road over the bridge, so he rode his horse straight down the bank into the water and swam across. From there he made straight for the place where he knew the Queen had gone. Trampled earth showed the battleground, and soon he was riding hard on the tracks of the company going back to the castle. Suddenly the men in ambush sprang out on him and shot his horse down. Raging, Sir Lancelot came at them on foot with his huge sword. They all turned and ran.

Sir Lancelot tramped on, over ditches and through wet fields in his heavy armor, getting more and more angry. He heard the welcome sound of a horse, and a woodman's cart came down the path with two carters in it. It was one of the rules of etiquette that no knight could ride in a cart. Sir Lancelot was too angry to care. He asked the carters if they would drive him to the castle, two miles off. The driver refused. Sir Lancelot scrambled into the cart and gave the man such a blow with his mailed fist that he fell over backwards, dead. The other carter hastily said that he would drive the knight wherever he wanted, and so Sir Lancelot came to the castle.

The Queen and her ladies were sitting restlessly in a bay window, refusing all conversation with Sir

Meliagraunce and his men, watching and waiting for Sir Lancelot. Up the winding approach from the woods to the castle gates came a horse and cart, and as they watched it, the Queen gave a cry, for she saw standing up in the cart an armed knight. She sprang up, and her ladies pressed to the window. "How lucky I am that he is my friend!" she cried.

Sir Lancelot arrived, alone, at the castle gate. Lifting his visor, he roared in a voice that rang over the wall and in all the windows: "Where are you, false Meliagraunce? Come out, you traitor, you and all your gang, for I am here, Sir Lancelot du Lac, to fight with you all." He seized the little gate and hurled it back on the porter who was hurrying down to lock it, and struck the man under the ear so that he broke his neck and killed him. He stepped into the archway, and then into the courtyard, and every one hid from him and kept dead quiet. He held the entire castle at bay.

Sir Meliagraunce was terrified. He ran to the Queen while Sir Lancelot raged in the courtyard and begged her to save him from Sir Lancelot. The Queen went swiftly down the winding stairs and out into the courtyard and took Sir Lancelot by both hands. He was still shouting for the traitor knight to come out and face him. The Queen laughed gently at him, thanked him for his coming and said: "The knight is sorely regretting this entire misadventure that he has embarked on."

Sir Lancelot, still half angry about his dead horse, answered gruffly: "Madam, if I had known you had made up with him so easily, I wouldn't have made such haste to get to you."

The Queen held his arm and smiled at him. "Why do you say that? Are you sorry you have done so well? You know I never made up with him because I liked him, but to stop a brawl and a scandal."

"Madam, no one except my lord King Arthur and you could stop me from killing Sir Meliagraunce before I go away."

"I know that well," she answered gently. "You shall have everything arranged as you decide."

Sir Lancelot's anger died, and he smiled back at her. "Madam, so long as you are pleased, it pleases me," and they went upstairs together to confront Sir Meliagraunce.

Trial by battle was arranged, eight days from then, in the fields beside Westminster. Sir Meliagraunce withdrew, heavy-hearted, bent on getting out of it by one means or another. Sir Lancelot went to talk to the ten wounded knights, and after that everyone settled down to spend the day resting and looking after the sick men. The next day they would all return to Westminster.

Sir Meliagraunce invited Sir Lancelot to inspect the castle. He had made some arrangements beforehand, and on the tour Sir Lancelot stepped on a trapdoor and fell into a deep cellar onto a pile of straw. Sir Meliagraunce fastened the trapdoor and went back to his rooms. When inquiry was made, he professed to know nothing of the visitor's whereabouts, and everyone thought that Sir Lancelot had suddenly left the castle and gone back to Westminster. He often made these unexpected departures and arrivals, which were a safeguard in times of danger.

Meantime Sir Lavaine arrived, and next morning he escorted the Queen and her party back to court. When they arrived, the Queen was surprised not to find Sir Lancelot, but every one assumed he was on some business of his own.

But next day Sir Meliagraunce appeared, not looking at all like a man who was due to fight Sir Lancelot in a week. He was almost careless about his behavior to the Queen and swaggered about in a way that amazed everyone. He kept this up day after day, until the Queen became uneasy. She spoke to several knights, and everyone agreed that Sir Meliagraunce's behavior, combined with Sir Lancelot's absence, looked as if some mischief had been worked. Sir Lavaine asked for the privilege of fighting instead of the champion, if by any evil chance it should be necessary. The King granted it, saying he was sure some treachery had been done.

All this time Sir Lancelot was shut up in the dark dungeon without sight of day. Food and drink were brought to him by the wife of one of the castle officers, who tried, like all women who came in contact with Sir Lancelot, to make him unfaithful to his vow to the Queen. She offered to set him free if he would become her knight. Politely but persistently Sir Lancelot refused. He knew his vow represented the ideal of honor and knighthood. If he would break his vow to the Queen in order to fight for her, his fighting for her would have no truth.

On the morning of the battle day, the lady's heart gave way. She knew that if she kept Sir Lancelot prisoner he would hate her forever, and if she let him free in time he would at least remember her with goodwill for that.

So Sir Lancelot escaped, in the nick of time. The

heralds were sounding and Sir Lavaine was ready at his end of the ground, when there was a commotion in the crowd and the great horse and rider came thundering on to the field. Roars went up as he was recognized. Saluting the King, he told everyone in a loud voice how Sir Maliagraunce had trapped him. The cheering changed to howls and hisses, and the crowd prepared for another of Sir Lancelot's victories.

But Sir Meliagraunce was a trickster to the last. The heralds blew, the knights withdrew to their ends of the lists, lances were poised, the trumpet sounded, and they charged. Sir Meliagraunce slid off his horse, and Sir Lancelot dismounted and approached sword in hand. But Sir Meliagraunce refused to fight. He yielded himself in the most grovelling language that chivalry allowed, and called on Sir Lancelot as a fellow knight of the Round Table not to kill him. He had lost all the privileges of knighthood by kidnapping the Queen and trapping Sir Lancelot, and yet he claimed them now to save himself. Sir Lancelot hesitated. He could not bring himself to kill a man who crawled on the ground and would not get up and fight, but if he let him go, he knew he would be treacherous again.

"Get up, man," he exclaimed, "and fight!"

"Not I," replied Sir Meliagraunce, who was trading on Sir Lancelot's chivalry and knew he was safe while he refused to fight. "I will never get up until you agree that I have surrendered."

"Well, I will make you an offer," said Sir Lancelot. "I will take my helmet off, and all the armor down my left side, and I will have my left arm tied behind me, and I will fight you like that."

Sir Meliagraunce stood up. Such a handicap had never been heard of.

"My lord King Arthur," he shouted, "you heard this offer; remember it, because I am going to accept it. Have him disarmed and bound according to his own offer."

The King spoke uneasily to his friend: "You cannot mean that, Sir Lancelot. You spoke in heat. You cannot keep such terms."

"I will, my lord, for I never go back on my word."

Everyone's heart sank as the disarming began. Protests arose all around the field, and the King and Queen fell silent. Only the enemies of the King, Sir Mordred and Sir Agravaine, and the evil men who plotted with them, leaned forward and suddenly drew breath. If Lancelot were killed, who knew what chance for evil might open in the kingdom?

Sir Lancelot was ready, his head, neck, half his body, and his left leg were bare, and his arm was tied behind him. Most men could not even lift their swords with only one hand, still less use them. Sir Lancelot knew the odds against him were so heavy that the first encounter could settle it. He was not afraid. Sir Meliagraunce rushed in. Sir Lancelot sprang aside swinging as he leaped, and there was a crash. Sir Lancelot stood waiting to be unbound, and men dragged Sir Meliagraunce off the field. His head and helmet were split in two.

Roar upon roar went up from the crowd. Sir Mordred and Sir Agravaine sat back and waited for another day.

CHAPTER 19

The Civil War

❦

IN SPITE OF THE GREAT DEEDS BY SIR LANCELOT and others, the Round Table was breaking down. The ideal of brotherhood and justice formed by King Arthur had been maintained for more than thirty years. The glory of the Round Table was such that in every generation, wherever men are moved by acts of love, brotherhood, and self-sacrifice, the life of King Arthur and the Round Table springs up again in their minds.

The final breakdown was caused by war between the King and Sir Lancelot. This tragedy was brought about by the Orkney clan, who fed their great anger until the greatest knights in Britain were all slain. The Orkney men were the sons of King Arthur's sister Morgause, Queen of Orkney, married to King Lot, who had been killed in war. The head of it was Gawaine, and under him were his brothers Gaheris, Agravaine, and Gareth, and Mordred, his half-brother, and all their relations. They were ambitious men, who wanted power rather than justice. They were jealous of any man greater than themselves, and especially the King's right-hand man, Sir Lancelot. To them he was a Frenchman who, by a hold on the Queen, had wormed his way into power and position that should be theirs. They were determined to bring down Sir Lancelot and the Queen at any cost, by lies and hate if a true opportunity did not arise. Only Gawaine and Gareth were exceptions.

But the rest of the clan were full of hate. Their leaders were Agravaine and Mordred. Now Sir Agravaine called a family council. He began by saying that Sir Lancelot was plotting to make himself king with the Queen's help, and that it was the clan's duty as relatives of King Arthur to defend him.

The result was that Sir Mordred, Sir Agravaine, and twelve kindred knights of the Round Table caught Sir Lancelot unarmed in an ambush in the palace. He was alone with the Queen and had no armor on, with only his sword. The door was locked, and the fourteen stood in the passage outside. They called on him to come out as a traitor and be taken. Both Sir Lancelot and the Queen knew that if the Orkney knights dared to do this in the palace itself, it was an open declaration of war. Sir Lancelot was desperately afraid for the Queen. If he were killed, the traitor clan would burn her alive.

"Now I would sooner have my armor on me than be lord of all Christendom," he said.

The enemy knights were preparing to break in the door. Lancelot called to them and said he was going to open. The Queen stood behind the door and Lancelot opened it a little. Sir Colegrevaunce rushed in and the Queen slammed the door and bolted it. Lancelot sprang on Sir Colegrevaunce and with one blow of his bare fist broke his neck. He and the Queen got the armor off the dead man, and laced it on Sir Lancelot. Then the Queen hid and Sir Lancelot threw open the door. At the first stroke he killed Sir Agravaine, and one after another all the rest. But unfortunately, when Sir Agravaine fell, Sir Mordred fled, sure now of being sole leader of the clan. Now he has the ill fame of bringing about the ruin of the kingdom.

Sir Lancelot stood breathing hard among the slain. Thirteen knights of the King's Round Table killed in his own palace! However true a friend he was, the King would have to punish Sir Lancelot for this. He left

THE QUEEN STOOD BEHIND THE DOOR AND
LANCELOT OPENED IT A LITTLE.

the Queen, who fully understood the seriousness of the situation, promising her his support in all dangers that might be coming, and went back to his own apartments. There he called an urgent council of his own Benwick clan. Ector, Bors, Lionel, and many others, including Lavaine of Astolat, all attended the meeting.

When they had all heard the story, Sir Bors said. "We have received much good with you and much honor. We will take the ill with you as we have taken the good." They all agreed too that he must stand by the Queen. Mischief was afoot, and they knew it would strike first at her.

"So, my fair lords, my kin, and my friends," said Sir Lancelot, knowing that it was possible that civil war might break out, "what will you do?"

"We will do as you will do," replied Sir Bors.

So Sir Lancelot outlined his plan and they filled in the details.

Meanwhile Sir Mordred and Sir Gawaine led their clan to demand an audience of the King. They told him that Sir Agravaine and twelve members of their family had caught Sir Lancelot plotting with the Queen and had been killed for their pains. They demanded that the Queen should be burned and Sir Lancelot outlawed.

The King heard them out, with his heart breaking. The Orkney men had beaten him at last. For years
they had been gnawing at the foundations of order, justice, and love by indifference, violent angers, and lies.
Now they had succeeded and had brought down the
King's work. The King knew that the Orkneys were too
powerful to be ignored. Thirteen Round Table knights of
their clan killed by Sir Lancelot had to be avenged. But
the King was certain that Mordred had worked some
trick. The triumph showing in his pale face convinced
the King of it.

"Make ready," the King said in a voice they had
never heard, and he gave orders to arrest the Queen.

The next morning, as Sir Lancelot expected, Sir
Mordred carried out the first of his plans. The Queen
was led out to be burned. The Benwick ambush was
ready, and at the signal they fell upon the procession and
escort. Hardly a man escaped the fury of Sir Lancelot and
his companions. This first engagement of the war that
was to kill all the leaders of chivalry was, with the last
battle, the most bitter of all. Twenty-four knights were
killed, including Sir Gaheris and Sir Gareth, who fell by
Sir Lancelot's hand unknowingly in the confusion of
combat. Again Sir Mordred escaped, for he was not

among the escort.

The Queen stood trembling in her condemned criminal's smock, where her jailers had left her when they fled. Sir Lancelot rode to her and pulled her up behind him and told her to be of good cheer. The entire company rode off at top speed to Sir Lancelot's stronghold of Joyous Gard and did not stop until they clattered into its safekeeping and the **portcullis** clanged down behind the last man.

The country was in turmoil. The war began to take shape as men joined one side or the other. Every one feared and hated the Orkneys, and they did no good to the King's side. Yet the King held

PORTCULLIS
A heavy iron grating suspended by chains and lowered to block the gateway of a castle or fortified town.

men's vows of loyalty. The entire kingdom was split. Most of the northern lords and knights gathered at Joyous Gard to fight on Sir Lancelot's side.

In the meantime the death of Gaheris and Gareth turned Gawaine's last streak of goodness into deep hate, deeper even than Sir Mordred's. The preparations for war went on fast, and before summer was over the King's army marched on Joyous Gard.

They camped around the wall of the town, inside which the mighty castle towered over the houses. Sir

Lancelot was the finest soldier of his time, and he had not neglected his own stronghold.

The battle was fierce and noble knights on both sides fell. King Arthur looked for Sir Lancelot to slay him. Sir Lancelot took the King's blows but would not strike back. So Sir Bors faced King Arthur and struck him down. Sir Bors got off his horse, drew his sword and said to Sir Lancelot, "Sir, shall I end this war?" for he meant to slay the king. "Do not dare," said Sir Lancelot. "Touch him no more." Then he got off his horse and raised the King and said to him:

"My lord King, for the love of God end this fighting. Remember what I have done in many places, and how now I am rewarded with evil."

The King looked on his lifelong friend and tears broke out of his eyes. Sir Lancelot's courtesy was greater than any other man's. Then the King could no longer look on him and rode away, saying to himself, "Alas, alas, that ever this war began."

The battle went on for many days, breaking off with the fall of darkness and starting again in the morning. Sir Gawaine wounded Sir Bors very badly and was wounded himself, but no one succeeded in hurting Sir Lancelot. The King's forces gained nothing at all.

While this unsatisfactory series of battles was going on, a stern command came to the King from the Pope. News of the civil war and the threat to Queen Guenevere had reached the Pope, who sent the Bishop of Rochester with a sealed letter telling the King to take his wife back again and make peace with Sir Lancelot. The King returned to Camelot to receive the Pope's messenger. He would have made peace with Sir Lancelot gladly, but Sir Gawaine would not let him. The Orkneys threatened the King with civil war if the King made peace with Sir Lancelot. They agreed, however, to take back the Queen. Safe-conduct was granted to Sir Lancelot, and the Bishop took the message to Joyous Gard.

Sir Lancelot was suspicious that it was a trap by the Orkneys to get hold of the Queen, but the Bishop pledged his word and showed the Pope's order, and so Sir Lancelot let her go. He took a hundred knights, clothed in green velvet, their horses clothed in the same to the heels, every knight holding an olive branch. The Queen had twenty-four ladies following her dressed in the same way. Sir Lancelot was attended by twelve young nobles on chargers, dressed in white velvet with gold bands, with precious stones gleaming in their cloaks. Their horses' trappings were of white velvet. At their head rode the Queen and Sir Lancelot, both in cloth of gold.

Twenty-five years ago the young King had sent his friend Sir Lancelot to bring his bride Guenevere to Camelot, and they had come in the spring of youth and hope. Now that friend, veteran leader of the King's armies and an outlaw in his realm, brought the Queen under clouds of anger and suspicion back to a ruined court. They had all passed their youth, and now when achievement should have been growing under their feet, black loss and failure appeared.

Yet as King Arthur and Sir Lancelot met in each other's presence for the last time, they knew that they were stronger than these men who had beaten them by hate and trickery. Beaten them? No. They who had fought the twelve great battles that pushed out the invaders, who had seen the Holy Grail and angels, who had made Britain from end to end a land of peace and justice, could they be broken? They were forever greater than their enemies.

But at this moment they could do nothing. Sir Gawaine sat at the King's right hand, and the enemy filled every seat around him.

Sir Lancelot alighted and gave the Queen his

hand. They came to the royal throne and knelt before the King. He sat silent. Sir Lancelot rose, raised the Queen, and said in a voice for all to hear:

"My King, by the Pope's command and yours I have brought to you my lady the Queen, as is right. If there be any knight, of whatever rank, except yourself, who will dare to say that she is not true to you, I here myself, Sir Lancelot du Lac, will prove upon his body that she is."

Sir Gawaine sprang up and began wildly accusing him. He brought up the death of Gareth and Gaheris, and Sir Lancelot defended himself. Sir Gawaine clenched his fist and rejected all offers of peace. He declared, while the King sat silent, that Sir Lancelot was exiled, and had fifteen days to leave the country, and that wherever he went Sir Gawaine would follow him until one or other was dead.

Lancelot looked at the King. He sat like stone. The Queen stood motionless. Seconds passed. All three knew that the old life was broken and that the end had come. Patching up was useless.

Then Sir Lancelot sighed, the tears fell on his cheeks, and he said: "Most noble Britain, whom I have loved above all other realms! Here I won most of my

honor, and now that I must depart in this manner, I regret that I ever came here, to be thus shamefully banished, undeserved and for no good reason. In this realm I had honor. By me and mine the Round Table won more in honor than it ever did by any one of you." He returned Sir Gawaine's challenge and said he would answer his charge of treason wherever Sir Gawaine followed him. Then he turned to the Queen and there was silence in the hall.

"Madam, now I must leave you and this noble fellowship forever. And since it is so, I beseech you to pray for me, and I will pray for you. If any false tongues accuse you, my good lady, swiftly send me word. If any knight's hand under heaven may save you, I will save you." Slowly he kissed her, and then gave her into the King's hand. He turned, and the entire hall stood to mark his going, as many times in the past these same men had stood to cheer his victories. In silence, magnificent in cloth of gold, Sir Lancelot passed through them and out of the realm of Britain. And the king and all the court, every knight and lady, all wept as if they were out of their minds, except Sir Gawaine.

CHAPTER 20

The Departure of Sir Lancelot

❧

S IR LANCELOT CALLED ALL HIS KIN AND FRIENDS together in the hall of Joyous Gard. He renamed the castle Dolorous Gard and told them he was exiled and was going back to his lands in France. What would they do? They all decided to go with him. For they all knew that in Britain there would be no peace, but always quarrels and war, now that the fellowship of the Round Table was broken.

He offered each of them lands, for he was lord of great provinces in western and southern France. So they took ship at Cardiff and sailed to Benwick, which now is called Bayonne. There Sir Lancelot gave every man the lands he had promised. Then he set out through all his ter-

ritories to see their preparations for war. He knew that Sir Gawaine would come, and he meant to be ready for him.

Sure enough, in a few months Sir Gawaine and King Arthur sailed from Cardiff with an army. Sir Mordred was left as governor of the kingdom and protector of the Queen. In a few weeks the British force was ravaging Sir Lancelot's lands. In Benwick Sir Lancelot held a council of war. Sir Bors urged open combat. Sir Lionel urged waiting until the enemy had run out of food and then to attack them. They all insisted that there was to be no more sparing of the King and showing courtesy, as Sir Lancelot had done in Britain. Here they were on their own ground. King Arthur had invaded them and they wanted to be free to treat him as an enemy.

The result of the council was that an offer of peace was sent by the hand of a damsel and a dwarf to the King's camp. But when she had delivered her message, the King gave Sir Gawaine permission to answer her, and the peace offer was rejected.

The next morning Benwick was besieged. For six months the siege went on. Every day Sir Gawaine rode in front of the main gates and took on a knight in single combat, and he always won. There were skirmishes and jousts but no serious fighting, and the months dragged

EVERY DAY SIR GAWAINE RODE IN FRONT OF THE
MAIN GATE AND MADE HIS CHALLENGE.

on. Then Sir Lancelot agreed to joust with Sir Gawaine, who had defeated and wounded so many of his knights. They met at last, and the battle was long and hard. For three hours they fought, but in the end Sir Lancelot laid Sir Gawaine helpless on the ground. He drew back and left him. Sir Gawaine ground his teeth and shouted to him to finish him off, swearing that as soon as he was healed he would seek him out again. Sir Lancelot answered that he would be ready for him, but that he would not kill a helpless man.

Sir Gawaine was carried to his tent and lay there for three weeks while his wound healed. When he was well, he came out and challenged Sir Lancelot again. They fought again, and the result was the same. As Gawaine lay on the field, frantic with defeat and helplessness, he still brandished his sword and tried to stab Sir Lancelot, shouting defiance at him.

Sir Lancelot turned away, saying: "Whenever you can stand on your feet, I will fight you, but I will not strike a wounded man who cannot stand." He went back inside the city gates.

In his madness, Sir Gawaine refused to listen to any sense or persuasions from the King or his own friends. He did not care if the entire army perished of cold and hunger, so long as his thirst for revenge was satisfied. His only plan was to wait until his wound was healed, and then to fight Sir Lancelot again.

But meanwhile news came from Britain to King Arthur that brought the entire camp to its senses. Mordred had announced to the people of Britain that he had received news that the King and Sir Lancelot were dead and he therefore declared himself King, had been crowned and was about to force the Queen to marry him. She had shut herself up in the **Tower of London** and Mordred had surrounded it.

Gawaine and his grievances were forgotten. The siege was over. The King ordered his army to pack and make all speed for Britain.

TOWER OF LONDON
The ancient fortress of London, begun by the Romans.

CHAPTER 21

The Last Battle and the Death of Arthur

❦

S IR MORDRED WAS READY FOR THE KING'S return. The moment he had planned so long had come. It was he of whom Merlin had said on the day when Arthur won his sword Excalibur that a son of Arthur's sister would be the destruction of his kingdom. That prophecy was soon to come true.

News of the King's approach reached Mordred, and he prepared to resist him with a large force drawn up on the Dover beach. But King Arthur was so courageous that no one could stop him from landing, and his knights followed him fiercely. But in the landing, Sir Gawaine was mortally wounded. Sir Lancelot was in France, but before Sir Gawaine died, he made his peace

IT WAS MORDRED OF WHOM MERLIN HAD SAID THAT A SON OF
ARTHUR'S SISTER WOULD BE THE DESTRUCTUON OF HIS KINGDOM.

with Sir Lancelot, saying aloud to the King and all the
knights gathered around: "Through me and my pride
you have all this shame and trouble. If that noble knight
Sir Lancelot were with you here, this unhappy war would

never have begun, for he, through his nobility, held all your enemies in subjection." He asked for paper and wrote to Sir Lancelot, asking him to return to England to help the King and to see his tomb.

At noon he died, and the knights buried him in a chapel in Dover castle. Now only Mordred was left of the Orkney clan, King Arthur's own blood, who had destroyed his kingdom.

The next day there was another skirmish between the King's forces and Sir Mordred's that ended in the rebels retreating. Then both sides collected their forces for a decisive battle. Mordred's stronghold was Canterbury. The King's strength lay in the west, so he set out to march in that direction, gathering forces as he went. Where the last battle was fought we do not know. We only know that it was somewhere on a far west sea-coast and on a misty day.

On the night before the battle, King Arthur dreamed that Sir Gawaine came to him and warned him that if he fought Sir Mordred on the next day he would be killed as well as the enemy. He must make a treaty, postponing the battle for a month and offer Mordred whatever terms would make him agree. In a month Sir Lancelot would arrive, and joining with the King, they would defeat the rebels.

The King awoke and sent for his leaders and told them his dream. They all agreed to obey it. Sir Lucan and Sir Bedivere and two bishops were sent to Mordred's camp to offer terms. Finally Mordred agreed to make peace at the price of getting Cornwall and Kent immediately and being made King Arthur's heir to all of Britain. A meeting was arranged to sign the treaty between King Arthur and Mordred, with fourteen attendants each, on the plain between their two armies. Neither side trusted the other. Each side was instructed by its leader to be fully armed, and if a single sword were drawn on the enemy side, they were to rush into battle.

The King and Sir Mordred met, the treaty was signed, and wine was fetched to mark its signing. As they waited, a snake came out of a bush and stung a knight in the foot. He seized his sword to kill the snake, and instantly both suspicious armies blew their trumpets, drew swords, and rushed upon each other. Back and forth surged the armies. The rebels were driven back but fought every step, for they knew there would be no mercy for them. At last they found themselves trapped against the beach.

The cliffs rang with the slaughter, the trumpets of battle, the crash of the battle-axe, spear, and sword,

SIR GAWAINE SAID ALOUD TO THE KING AND ALL THE KNIGHTS
GATHERED AROUND, "THROUGH ME AND MY PRIDE YOU HAVE ALL
THIS SHAME AND TROUBLE."

the screams of horses, and the shouts of men. Thus they fought all the long day and never stopped until a hundred thousand noble knights were laid dead upon the cold earth.

Of all that mighty host, only two remained alive to stand beside the King, Sir Lucan and Sir Bedivere, and they were both wounded. "Where is that traitor Sir Mordred who has caused all this evil?" said the King, glaring around on the dead and gripping his sword Excalibur. Then he saw Sir Mordred leaning on his sword among a great heap of dead men. Sir Lucan tried to stop the King, reminding him of his dream and how his life had been spared so far, and that the day was his since there were three of them left, and of the enemy only Sir Mordred lived. But the King, with all his knights dead about his feet, would not now flinch.

"Come death, come life," he cried, "I see him yonder alone. He shall never escape my hand!" They ran at each other. The King's sword thrust right through Sir Mordred, who in his death agony hurled himself forward right against the hilt to strike the King on the helmet and pierce through to his head. They both fell; Mordred was dead and the King was desperately wounded.

His wound was deep. Sir Bedivere lifted him up

and carried him to a chapel near the battlefield. As they carried the King on that short journey, Sir Lucan died, and Sir Bedivere was left alone with the King. King Arthur felt his end was drawing near, and he remembered Excalibur, his sword. On one side of the blade was carved "Take me," and on the other "Cast me away." With that sword he had won and held the kingdom, and now the end was near.

He said to Sir Bedivere: "Take my good sword Excalibur, go with it to the water's edge and throw my sword into the water. Then come back and tell me what you saw."

Sir Bedivere took Excalibur and climbed down to the shore. All the way down, the magic and the worth of Excalibur worked in his mind, until he desired to possess it for his own. He half desired it for its value and beauty in precious stones, and half as a relic of the King. On the seashore he held the long blade in his hands, and the moonlight turned the bloodstains black and ran like sparks around his hand.

He did not throw it. He hid Excalibur under a stunted tree and went back to the King and told him he had done as he was told. Eagerly the King raised himself in his weakness. "What did you see?"

"'Sir, I saw nothing but dark waves."

The King stared at him and then realized the truth. "You have lied to me," he said. "Now go quickly and do what I told you. Spare not, but throw it in."

Sir Bedivere went again, but all the way he thought that the King was weak and dying, did not know what he was saying, and that it would be good for the future if the sword were saved. All the knights were killed, the King was dying, there would not be one trace or proof left of their greatness. The sword must be saved. He hid Excalibur again and went a second time to King Arthur in the ruined chapel.

"What did you see?"

"I saw the water lapping on the rocks and rippling in the reeds," answered Sir Bedivere.

Then the King raised up in majesty and wrath flashed in his eyes. "Ah, traitor and untrue, now you have betrayed me twice."

Sir Bedivere shrank back.

"Who would have thought that you who have been so dear and precious to me and called a noble knight, that you would betray me for the riches of this sword? Now go again quickly, for your long delay has put me in danger of my life, for I have taken cold. Unless you do as I tell you now, if ever I see you again I shall kill you with my own hands, for you would let me die for the sake of my rich sword."

Sir Bedivere turned and fled. He ran down the rocky path and stumbled over the stones to the tree, seized Excalibur, and hurled it far out over the water. But before Excalibur dipped in the surface, up arose an arm clothed in white silk and caught it by the hilt, brandished it three times, and drew it under in the sea.

The knight's hair rose upon his head. King Arthur heard his steps running and slipping on the path and knew before he spoke that he had been faithful the third time.

"Alas, help me get away," said the King, "for I am afraid I have stayed too long."

Sir Bedivere lifted the King on his shoulders and carried him down to the water. There they found a barge hung with black from bow to stern, crowded with figures draped and veiled in black, and among them a crowned Queen with two other queens, all three veiled in black. From the barge rose a cry of grief as they approached.

"Now put me into the barge," said the King.

Sir Bedivere did so and the sorrowful figures laid

him down with his head in the Queen's lap.

As she took him she said: "Ah, my dear brother! Why have you stayed so long from me?"

The barge began to draw away from the shore, and Sir Bedivere realized that he was left alone, and behind him lay a hundred thousand dead. "My lord Arthur," he cried, "what will become of me, now that you are going and leaving me here alone?"

"Comfort yourself," answered the King from the barge, "and do as well as you can, for I can do no more good for you. I must go to Avalon to heal my grievous wound." The barge was moving away and his voice came faintly on the night air. "If you never hear of me again, pray for my soul."

Sir Bedivere stood still a long time, recalling many memories, until the barge became a black dot against the horizon that was rosy with dawn, and the sounds of wailing from across the sea finally died away.

Then he left the shore, climbed back on to the cliffs, and, turning away from the battleground, walked all night through the woods. In the early light he came to a chapel, and there he saw a hermit lying on the ground in prayer beside a new grave.

THE SORROWFUL FIGURES RECEIVED HIM AND LAID

HIM DOWN WITH HIS HEAD IN THE QUEEN'S LAP.

"Sir," said Sir Bedivere, "what man is buried here that you pray for so intently?"

"Fair son," answered the hermit, "I only know by guessing. This very night, at midnight, came a number of ladies who brought a dead man and prayed me to bury him."

"Alas," said Sir Bedivere, "that was my lord King Arthur who lies buried in this chapel." He fainted as he spoke. When he recovered, he asked the hermit if he might stay there always and serve him and pray for the soul of the King.

However, neither of them knew for certain what man lay buried there, nor where the barge had gone with the three queens. No man had known the secret of King Arthur's birth, and no man knew the secret of his end. The King said he was going to Avalon to be healed of his wound. And after he was healed? In the dark days of war and murder, robbery, and burning that came upon the land when Arthur's rule was gone, it was whispered that the King was not dead, that he had only gone to another place, and he would come again and set up again the rule of justice and right. Men said that in an unknown tomb in a chapel in the forests near Glastonbury there was a prophecy carved in crude letters, scarcely readable:

HIC JACET ARTHURUS,
REX QUONDAM REXQUE FUTURUS

(Here lies Arthur, King that was and King that shall be.)

CHAPTER 22

The Death of Guenevere and of Sir Lancelot

T HE LAST BATTLE HAD BEEN FOUGHT, AND ALL the ruling knights and lords of Britain had been killed. The King had vanished on his unknown destiny, and Britain had no ruler, no court, and no government. What of the Queen? She stayed in the Tower of London until the news came of the last battle. Then she put off her royal clothes and dressed in black, and with five ladies took their horses early one morning and slipped out of London at the moment the gates were opened. Disguised as nuns, they fled across Britain to the west, to Amesbury in Wiltshire, where there was an abbey.

The Queen became a nun, put on the black-and-white **habit**, and led the strictest life in the convent. She showed such constancy and goodness, combined with the strength of her character, and knowledge of how to rule, that in time she was made head of the convent. There she stayed until the end of her life. But there was one more incident awaiting her from the stormy world outside.

HABIT
Clothing worn to show a religious calling in life.

Sir Lancelot received the letter written by Sir Gawaine on his deathbed, telling him of Mordred's treachery and asking him to come at once to help the King and rescue the Queen. He did not know about the last battle. He and Sir Bors at once gathered the fighting force of their family from all over France and came with speed to Britain. They landed at Dover, where they were told the news of the last battle and the collapse of the kingdom.

Sir Lancelot made his peace with the dead Gawaine and knelt for long hours by his tomb. With that the feud was healed, and Sir Lancelot turned to his next duty. He summoned all his followers and told them that he was going to look for the Queen. If he did not return in fifteen days, they were to go home. He thanked them for their support. Sir Bors came to him after the council and urged him to take a few friends with him, as Britain was fast becoming a dangerous country again with bandits on the roads. But Sir Lancelot was thinking of other things and answered: "Stay here, for I shall go alone on my journey."

He knew where the Queen would have hidden, and he rode straight there. He knocked at the gate, and though no man was allowed inside the nunnery, when the nuns at the gate saw Sir Lancelot, they backed away from the gate and left it open. In he walked and passed unchallenged through courtyard after courtyard, the nuns gasping at the sight of him and silently gliding away. He asked one where to find the Queen, and she pointed without speaking. He came around a corner, saw her and stood still.

When Queen Guenevere saw him there, she fainted three times. Her nuns brought a seat, and Sir Lancelot stood still, waiting. When the Queen could speak, the nuns brought him to her. She said to them all and to him, "Through this man and me has all this war happened, and the deaths of the noblest knights of the world, and through us is my most noble lord slain. Therefore, Sir Lancelot, I demand and beg of you, for the sake of all the love that was between us, that you never see me face to face again. For God's sake, never come near me again. Go back to your kingdom, and keep it well from war and harm, for well as I have loved you in the past, my heart can no longer bear the strain of seeing you."

"Now, my beloved," said Sir Lancelot, "do you want me to go away to my country? That I will never do, for I shall never betray all the promises I have made to you. But the same life you have taken to, I will take too, and to pray especially for you."

"Ah, Sir Lancelot, if you would do it and keep to it!" said the Queen.

"Madam, never yet did you know me to break my promise. In you I have had my earthly joy, and if I had found you so disposed, I had thought of taking you back to my own kingdom. But since I find you have chosen this life, I choose it too. So, madam, I pray you, kiss me once again and never more."

"No, I will never do that," said the Queen, and so they parted.

Sir Lancelot rode all day and all night, until he heard a bell ringing in the forest. He followed it and found the chapel where Sir Bedivere lived with the hermit, and there he stayed and became a hermit with them.

Meantime at Dover his friends were growing

anxious. Sir Lionel rode to London to look for him and was killed by bandits on the road. Sir Bors decided to send the army home, and then he, with Sir Lancelot's brother, Sir Ector, set out in search. They were led by mysterious fate to the very hermitage where Sir Lancelot was, and there they stayed and lived a holy life with the others.

Six years passed and one night a vision came to Sir Lancelot in the night that he should go to the Queen. In the morning he got ready. He and his friends walked to Amesbury, and when they arrived at the nunnery, they found that the Queen had died half an hour before they came. With a hundred torches burning around the bier, they escorted the Queen for the last time on the journey to Glastonbury.

After she was laid in the earth, Sir Lancelot did not live more than six weeks. Neither food nor drink interested him, and although the loving Sir Bors and all his friends tended him, he faded before their eyes. He scarcely slept at all and was generally found beside the Queen's tomb, cheerful but not interested in living. Soon he was too weak to get up from bed, and he made Sir Bors promise to take him all the way north to Joyous Gard and bury him there.

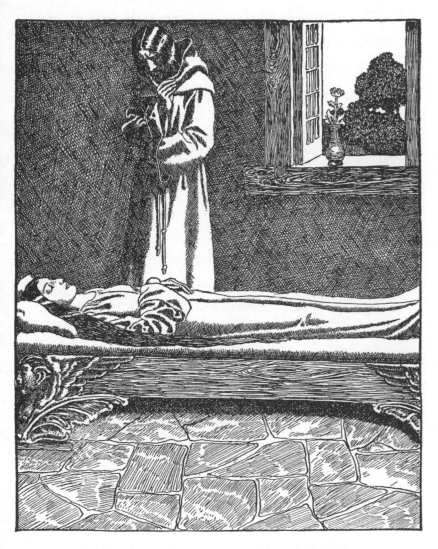

THEY FOUND THAT THE QUEEN HAD DIED HALF
AN HOUR BEFORE THEY CAME.

One night Sir Ector woke suddenly and by impulse went to Sir Lancelot's cell. He found him dead, and smiling.

"Ah, Lancelot!" he said. "You were the head of all knights. You were never matched. You were the most courteous knight, the truest friend, the truest lover that ever loved a woman, the kindest man that ever came among a company of knights, the gentlest man that ever ate in hall among ladies, and the sternest knight to your enemies that ever struck with a sword."

After the burial of Sir Lancelot, Sir Bedivere stayed in the hermitage for the rest of his life, but Sir Bors and Sir Ector went home to France to their own lands. From there they went on crusades to the Holy Land, where in the end they were killed fighting against the Saracens.